Also by Davy Rothbart

*Found: The Best Lost, Tossed, and Forgotten
Items from Around the World*

THE LONE SURFER OF MONTANA, KANSAS

STORIES

DAVY ROTHBART

A TOUCHSTONE BOOK
PUBLISHED BY SIMON & SCHUSTER
New York   London   Toronto   Sydney

TOUCHSTONE
Rockefeller Center
1230 Avenue of the Americas
New York, NY 10020

First Touchstone Edition 2005

TOUCHSTONE and colophon are registered trademarks
of Simon & Schuster, Inc.

For information regarding special discounts for bulk purchases,
please contact Simon & Schuster Special Sales at 1-800-456-6798
or business@simonandschuster.com.

Designed by Jan Pisciotta and Paul Hornschemeier

Manufactured in the United States of America

10   9   8   7   6   5   4   3   2   1

Library of Congress Cataloging-in-Publication Data
  Rothbart, Davy.
      The lone surfer of Montana, Kansas : stories / Davy Rothbart.
          p. cm.
      "A Touchstone book."
        I. Title.
   PS3618.0864 L66   2005
   913'.6—dc22   2005048652

ISBN-13: 978-0-7432-6305-4
ISBN-10:   0-7432-6305-7

This Is For

Rachel, Maggie, Bonnie, Adriane, Nicole, Liz, Kerry, Emilie, Samantha, Sarah, and Shade.

This Is Also For

My doggs—you know who the fuck you are.

Contents

LIE BIG

ONE TIME MITEY-MIKE tripped a silent alarm in a jewelry store. It was three-thirty in the morning. The cops came.

He told me about this the next day.

Mitey-Mike saw the cops at the front window. He didn't try to run or hide. He walked right up to them. "Hey!" he shouted through the glass. "You have to go around back. Through the alley. The back door. I don't have the key to this one." He met them at the back door—the door he'd jimmied—and invited them in. "I'll get some coffee going," he said. "Caf or decaf?"

The cops wanted to know who he was. There were four of them. They said they were responding to an alarm.

"I'm Jerry's nephew," Mitey-Mike told them. "Come on in. Give yourselves a break. We've got chairs in here. There's coffee if you want. I'm going to have coffee. Actually, I'm going to have a beer. You know what I mean? A late-night beer. There's beer in the basement. Here, let me get some lights on."

He roamed around the store looking for the light

switches. Three of the cops sat down in chairs; the fourth remained standing and watched him. Mitey-Mike found the lights. He turned them on. He walked back over to the cops. "Listen here," he said to the cop who was standing, "have a seat. *Mi casa, su casa.*" He brought a chair over. These were the chairs customers sat in to peer into the jewelry cases and try on rings and bracelets and talk to the jewelers. It was that kind of store. The cop finally sat down. "Now what can I get for you guys?" said Mitey-Mike. "How 'bout a beer?"

One of the cops said, "We'd like to see some ID, please."

Mitey-Mike stared at him, then stared at each of them, and laughed. "You mean Jerry didn't tell you about the boat?" He paused. He looked them in the eyes. "The boat. You know about the boat, right?" He laughed again. "You guys don't know about the boat. You probably have no idea why I'm here."

He pulled a chair up for himself. "This was the big weekend," he said. "Jerry decided it was time. Well, god-damn, he's been dating the girl the better part of three years. It was more than time. You know her? Nika? The surgeon? No? Okay. Anyway, he took her up to Drum-mond Island for the weekend. He's got the place there. The beach house. Comfy, but there's spiders. He got me to come along. Anne, too. He wanted us to videotape it when he popped the question. The idea was, we'll have the cam-era out and be messing with it. On the beach. Filming the sunset. Then he'll get down on one knee."

The cops looked on with a mixture of bafflement, boredom, and lingering suspicion.

"The ring," Mitey-Mike continued. "Now Jerry's got some nice rings right here in the shop. In fact, if you'd like, you're welcome to try some on. Look around. Let me know what catches your eye. But the point is, Nika used to work here. Before med school. She knows the goddamn inventory. Jerry's not going to just pluck something out of the case. It's got to be special. It *was* special. Listen.

"They went to Morocco in February. Sure, just leave me here alone, Jerry, leave me here all alone to run things during Valentine's Day rush. Thanks a *lot*, Jerry. So. They're in Marrakech. The marketplace. Crazy narrow streets. Thousands of twists and turns. I saw pictures. Well, what happens is, they get separated from each other in there. Jerry's not worried—Nika's a big girl, she can take care of herself, she can find her way back to the hotel. This is perfect, though. Jerry can look for a ring in secret. He finds this old-man jeweler, a nomad—they call them Blue Men—they're tribal peoples, desert folk. This old guy makes these rings, okay? You know what a quarter-cusp is?" Mitey-Mike leaned in toward the cop nearest him. "Here, let me see your hand."

"We can't stay long," said the cop. His walkie-talkie buzzed with radio traffic.

"Okay. Fast forward, fast forward. Listen," said Mitey-Mike, "Jerry's all ready to give her the ring. This was the big weekend. But this morning we go out in the boat, me and Jerry, and yeah, you guessed it. *The boat fucking flips.*

Now this is the weird part. We'd hit something underwater. That's what flipped us. But guess what it was. I'll tell you. It was a *car*, an *automobile*—for example, what you'd drive to the market in or pile full of kids for their Saturday morning soccer game. We hit a car with his boat. Jerry had the ring in his coat pocket. Well, that's gone. My wallet's gone, too, but that stuff's easy to replace."

The cop who was last to sit down now stood. "What'd he do," the cop chuckled, "send you all the way back down here to get another ring?"

"Yes, sir. And his scuba gear."

The cop looked at him. "I thought the guy who owned this place was named Maynard."

"Maynard?" said Mitey-Mike. "Maynard's just the manager. He's a moron. No, he's a nice guy. But he's terrible with the books. You know what, though. He saved Jerry's life once." He raised his eyebrows. "Australia. Sharks."

At this point, in recounting the story to me, Mitey-Mike fell silent. We were shooting baskets at Wheeler Park, down by the old train station. "Well, what happened?" I asked him.

"What do you mean?"

"What do you mean, 'what do you mean?' What happened next?"

"Nothing. They left. I told them I'd close up. I told them to stop by during business hours and take a look at our fine selection." Mitey-Mike reached into his jeans with both hands and pulled a long gold chain from each pocket. "Here," he said. "Take your pick."

I looked at him.

"There's a lesson in this," he said.

"What's that?"

He bounced the basketball and shot from thirty feet, an airball that rolled all the way to the grass. *"Swish!"* he said. He grinned at me. "Lie big."

MITEY-MIKE ALWAYS LIED BIG. He told marvelous lies, outlandish lies, terrible and astounding lies, sad and dangerous lies, silly lies, beautiful, exquisite and thunderous lies. He lied, mostly, to get out of trouble, but often he lied for no reason at all. Times when truth would have sufficed, when a small lie would have done the job, he still lied big. Preposterous lies, he said, had more style. He lied to teachers and cops, to employers, to girlfriends, and even to me, his best friend. Once, twenty minutes late to pick me up from Bell's Pizza, where we both worked, he arrived with a story of taking his cousin's ferret on an emergency trip to the vet.

"Look, don't worry about it," I said.

"I *am* worried," he said. "I'm worried about little Smokey. I don't know if the poor rascal's gonna make it through the night. They think he was poisoned. What kind of creep would poison a little kid's ferret?"

Nothing was too sacred to use for material. In high

school, I'd heard him explain to a math teacher after class why he hadn't brought his homework in. His brother in Rhode Island, Mitey-Mike said, had called him the night before, suicidal. Mitey-Mike spoke very softly and slowly and stared at his hands. "I could hear that his voice was funny," he said. "Not funny like upset, just weird-sounding, and I asked him why, and he told me, well, the gun was in his mouth."

Mitey-Mike sometimes said that as an authority on lying it was important to pass his knowledge on to others, and by others he meant me. He said that the best lies didn't have to make sense and didn't have to relate directly to what you were lying about—if something disastrous had really just happened to you, it's unlikely you'd be able to explain yourself clearly. One of his favorite strategies was to appear badly shaken and cry out in deep, inexpressible sorrow, "The *dogs*. They were shitting *everywhere*. They just kept shitting and shitting!" He believed there were other can't-miss lines, like any that involved spilling a steaming-hot drink into your own lap and burning your penis. No one in history had ever been asked to supply a doctor's note for a burnt penis.

Mitey-Mike always cautioned me not to say too much, not to overexplain. People who are telling the truth, he said, never feel the need to go into too much detail, though there were also times, he acknowledged, when an incredible story was necessary, like when he'd been caught inside the jewelry store.

Never back down from a lie, Mitey-Mike instructed me. Whenever someone challenged him, he'd respond with wounded ferocity, with such blazing and forceful conviction that people either believed him or gave in to the lie rather than continue the argument. He was a bully in that way. On the basketball court, if his team scored the first point of the game, he'd call out the score, "Four-nothing."

Someone on the other team would protest. "Four? That's the first bucket."

Mitey-Mike's eyes would go wide and he'd howl, "No fucking *way!* I scored twice myself,"—he'd point at me— "and my man right here scored one. That's three-nothing. Check it up."

Sometimes the lies turned ugly. Mitey-Mike lied to his girlfriends. He usually had two or three girlfriends at the same time. I saw the hurt in their faces when he lied to them—they knew he was lying but pretended to themselves and to him that they didn't. Mitey-Mike found ways to make me complicit in his lies. He'd leave one girl's house and pick me up at my grandma's, and together we'd drive over to another one of his girlfriends' houses. She'd be upset that he was an hour and a half late, and he'd explain that we'd been giving my grandma a bath. The girl would look at me and I'd nod gravely and explain, "She gets sores if we don't get her out of bed and into the tub every few days." Then Mitey-Mike would drop me off back at my house and speed away with the girl.

You might think I'd get tired of all the lies but I never

did. Each sad and damaging lie he told was followed by thirty wild, joyous, sprawling, magical lies. It was a glorious feeling to be in cahoots with him, to be backstage, behind the curtain, on the side of *knowing*, and watch him weave his brilliant tapestries. People delighted in him and his power over them was mesmerizing.

From fifth grade on, Mitey-Mike was my best friend and really my only friend—when I hung out with other people he got jealous and brooded around town until I abandoned my new friends and came back to him. In me he had a sidekick, someone to witness all of his impossible feats; in turn, he provided me with adventure and a way to meet girls. We were a pretty good team for about fourteen years. But you know how it is. Things fall apart.

FIRST, KATY APPEARED. She came into Bell's Pizza one night after we'd already closed, a shy, beautiful, pale-skinned girl with green hair, wearing big jeans and a Joe Dumars jersey. I was up front counting out the register; Mitey-Mike was in back mopping out the walk-in cooler—if we'd been reversed, things might have unfolded differently. I gave Katy two free slices of pizza and asked for her phone number; within a couple of weeks we were a couple.

My love for Katy was sharp and aching. When she wasn't right next to me I was miserable. Even when we were lying close together or, you know, making with the love, I still couldn't seem to get close enough. I'd always imagined that Mitey-Mike would disapprove when I finally found a girl to be with because I'd be less available to him, but he was cool about Katy. He said it made him feel good to see me so wrapped up in someone. He seemed genuinely happy for me. A couple of weekends in a row he covered my shifts so Katy and I could go camping up north.

One night in August I got off work early, before midnight, and went looking for Mitey-Mike to see if he wanted to play some basketball. Through the front window of his house, in the glow from the TV, I saw him making out with a girl on the living room floor. I'd actually happened upon this type of scene at his house a couple of times before and had jetted, but this time I stayed for a moment because the Tigers game was on the TV and I could see that Detroit had runners at second and third with nobody out. I must have gotten caught up in the game because a couple of minutes later I realized all of a sudden that Mitey-Mike and the girl were sitting up and staring at me. You know how you can look at something and not really see it for what it is, and then there's this tremor and things flip into place? For about a second and, oh, maybe another third of a second, it was just Mitey-Mike and a girl—then things popped into focus, and it was Mitey-Mike and Katy.

A great, deafening roaring sound filled my ears; blood banged its way through my neck and my arms; my entire body buzzed like I'd grabbed hold of a downed power line. The world came to me in a series of fade-ins and fade-outs. I remember running as hard as I could, chased by Mitey-Mike. The next thing I knew I was sitting on the front porch of a house somewhere, Mitey-Mike standing over me, his face a foot away. I was yelling at him and he was yelling back. At some point the porch light turned on and an old man appeared in the doorway. "The fuck you looking at!" Mitey-Mike screamed at the guy. Next we were running again, all the way through downtown, and then we were standing on the basketball court at Wheeler Park, heaving for breath and drenched in sweat.

Mitey-Mike shook me by the shoulders. "Look at me," he said. "Look at me! You think you know what you saw—but you don't! You don't!"

I pushed him away from me and screeched for him to fuck off.

He shook me again. "You need to chill the fuck out! I was giving her a back rub! Do you understand? A silly fucking back rub!"

Maybe I was crying, I don't know. I sagged away. "Can you tell me the truth," I said. My head pounded. "It's me, okay? Come on, now. It's me. Just tell me what's happening. I just want to know what's happening."

"Nothing's happening," he said. "We're here at the park. We're talking. Katy's probably wondering where the hell we are."

I tore at my forehead and my cheeks. "Mike, I saw, okay? I saw is all. You don't have to make anything up. I saw what I saw. I saw you guys."

Mitey-Mike was quiet for a bit. The night pulsed. Finally he said, "Okay, listen. You want to hear everything, I'll tell you. I asked Katy to come over for a reason. I asked her to bring me something specific over, some medicine, some hydrocortisone cream. Listen to me! She was helping me put it on. Earlier today—listen to me! Earlier today, I spilled bleach on myself. Listen! I burnt my penis."

Memory is strange. I don't remember punching him, I just remember him saying that last thing, then looking up at me with his face covered in blood. "You're bleeding," I said, surprised by it. Then I turned and ran.

For about six months my dad had been in my ear, asking me to come out to Sacramento and help him with his business. He sold trampolines to rich people. A week later I was out there learning the ropes.

IN LATE DECEMBER, two days before the new year, Mitey-Mike was killed in an accident. It was the kind of spectacular tale he might have come up with himself after missing a week of work. What happened was he was walking his neighbor's dog in a field near his house and he got hit by an airplane. A little two-man Cessna. Both pilots died and so did Mitey-Mike, but the dog lived. Hassan, my old boss at Bell's Pizza, explained everything. I'd never heard him so upset. "Will you come back for the funeral?" he asked me. I told him I didn't know.

Katy called the next day, New Year's Eve. She was crying. We talked for a long time. She told me she'd loved Mitey-Mike; I told her I'd loved him, too. She said they'd found an apartment together in Ypsilanti and they were supposed to move in on the first of February. They'd bought some furnishings already—drapes and a furry toilet-seat cover.

"What are you gonna do?" I asked her.

"I don't know," she said. "I was thinking of moving out there to California."

"Here?"

"Well, to L.A. You remember Jenna? She lives there."

"It'd be nice to have you out here. L.A.'s not too far from here."

"Yeah. That would be nice." She began to cry again.

"You know what I'm wearing," I said, "I'm wearing that gold necklace he gave me. Remember the long gold chain he gave me? From when he broke into that jewelry store? He had one that matched it. Remember?"

Katy said, "I know which necklace you're talking about."

"Yeah, I wear it every day. I guess I have since he gave it to me." I wrapped the long end of it around my fingers and through them. "Katy, you know the jewelry store story, right? How he broke in and there was a silent alarm and the cops came?"

"I know that story," she said. "That's your favorite Mitey-Mike story. You love that story. You always tell that story. You told me that story before I even met him."

"Yeah. It's a good story."

"Well, he made it up. Last week he told me. No, two weeks ago. He got that necklace at Bunky's on Michigan Avenue. His necklace, too, the one that matched. He traded his old Nintendo for them. And a bunch of games." She took a long, staggered breath. Someone else was saying something to her in the background. "Listen," she said, "I got to go. Let's talk later. Can we talk some more? Can we talk tomorrow? I think we should keep talking."

My head and my hands felt light. "Call me tomorrow," I said.

"Okay. 'Bye then. Happy New Year's."

"Okay," I said. "Okay. Okay. Happy New Year."

FIRST SNOW

THAT FALL AND ON INTO WINTER it was a joke among the other five of us on our roadside crew, something we'd say to cement the bonds between one another and keep Maurice safely outside our little circle. Colin, who was in for robbery and who was, at twenty-three, the oldest of us and by far the most clever, came up with the catchphrase.

It started one morning as we rode in the back of the van on our way to a cleanup site, when Maurice said, "Take one step toward Allah and he'll take two steps toward you." When he spoke we could never be sure if he was directing his words at us or talking to himself, so quiet was his voice, his gaze always set off to the side or down at his feet. The rest of us looked around at one another, sneering at this bit of wisdom so early in the day. In us an anger still simmered, the anger of those who have been on the inside for only a couple of months, the anger of incredulity that someone would dare to take you away from your life and put you behind a twenty-foot barbed-wire fence. We were white; we were young. Allah was as much our friend as the cops who had taken us in.

For three hours that morning we picked up trash and

rehearsed what we knew of proud silences and defiant expressions. Once or twice a car zoomed past with a girl inside, dark hair whipping in the wind, still parading a summer tan in her bikini top even though by then it was late September and cold in Michigan, and we shouted after her and gave chase for a giddy half-second before Greider, the guard, brought us to a stop by raising up his club. We had no doubt that he'd use it. Maurice worked on his own, a little bit away from us.

At noon we ate sandwiches in the back of the van; Greider dozed up front with a newspaper over his face, a curtain of wire mesh and Plexiglas dividing us. I don't know if Colin had spent the entire morning cooking this up or if he divined it in that moment, but once he'd finished his lunch, he entertained himself by faking sudden hard punches at Maurice. At each feigned blow Maurice flinched and seemed to draw back further into himself; he was so mute and withdrawn it was hard to tell when Colin spoke whether Maurice was ignoring him or simply didn't hear. "Hey, guys, I got one for you," Colin said, looking around and gathering his audience the way he always did before delivering a line he knew we would prize. "Check it out, you take one step toward Maurice, he takes two steps *away* from you."

We all laughed; maybe I laughed the loudest, I don't know. The laughter of men on the inside is sad and cruel. Joyous laughter, exuberance, exhilaration—these had no place in our lives at Galloway Lake Detention Center. I've been in a lot of places in the years since and some of them were a lot worse, dangerous, completely devoid of humor in any form; in some prisons I have also seen, on occasion, a bright twinkle in the eyes of some of the older guys that bordered on real merriment, but it was always followed with the same wistful and lost look. Every emotion can basically be experienced in two distinct ways: as felt in freedom, and as felt in shackles. There is happiness behind bars, but it is always chained to something large and immovable. Anger, on the inside, has no place to go. Even loneliness, and grief, and loss, cannot be felt as fully in prison as when you are free. At least for the five of us, targeting Maurice, laughing at his expense, suspended the monotony of our rage. The little quick breaths that came with our snickering seemed to relieve for a moment the pressure mounting inside us.

We spent six mornings and afternoons a week along one sixteen-mile stretch of I-94, roaming the high dry median weeds and the steep marshy embankments, picking up refuse, items so unwanted and vile that highway motorists couldn't bear to keep them in their cars until they reached a trash can at home. We filled hundreds of blue plastic bags with fast-food wrappers and diapers, pop cans rattling with bees, jagged debris left from high-speed collisions; weeks passed and still the joke had not lost its luster. "Take one step toward Maurice," Justin or Nick or John Jay might say once we were back in the back of the van with the bags of garbage we'd collected that day, and we'd all crack up before they even finished. Maurice would stare ahead as if he was trying to fade into nothing. Sometimes he'd turn away. The joke gave a rhythm and shape to our days.

Galloway Lake was not really even a prison so much as a small work camp for first- and second-time serious offenders. For me, and for most of us, it was our first time inside, so when the air got colder and the leaves changed to yellow and orange and red, then to brown, and at last detached themselves and fell away, and we knew winter was on its way, a certain desperation latched on to our hearts. It's a peculiar sensation, that first change of seasons when you're locked up. You begin to understand that while time is frozen for you, it continues on for the rest of the world. Pain constricts your insides. There's an inescapable heat and ache at your temples. It becomes hard to breathe. I know all of us felt it, because our attacks on Maurice came with renewed viciousness and vigor. We never laid a hand on him—Greider's presence prevented that—but we spat abuse in his face. I remember Nick was the most relentless. Nick told me once that I was. Through it all, I knew that Maurice had been chosen as our victim not only because he was black, and different from us in countless other ways, but because he was the weakest, and weakness, above all things, could not be tolerated. It is no defense, but I offer it as a fact: had I been the weakest, they would have preyed on me.

Maurice, though, Maurice was exceptionally weak. He was just a few inches over five feet, so slight as to resemble a child. He wore big glasses that he cleaned every few minutes by rubbing spit on the thick lenses before drying them with a fold of his pant leg. Some guys retained a quiet dignity in backing away from confrontation. You had the sense that everything you said to them went unnoticed. Maurice, on the other hand, seemed to exist in a state of constant fear and agitation. He trembled at our approach. Insults stung him visibly. The only reason he did not retaliate was because he was so afraid.

Thanksgiving passed, a cold holiday. We missed the turkey dinner because our van ran out of gas a mile from Galloway Lake and Greider had to radio for another van. December came, and with it gray skies and even colder days. Colin said that when it got too cold they'd take us off highway cleanup and put us to work in the kitchen or in the laundry room, but all they did was issue us warmer outfits and gloves. In the colder weather there was less trash, since tossing things to the roadside required people first to roll down their windows. Sometimes we'd stretch out in a wide semicircle, Maurice off to the side a little, Greider watching us from the shoulder. We'd talk about football and girls we used to know, our eyes flickering over the flashes of passing traffic. I recall thinking once that to the people speeding by, on their way to school or work in the morning, or in the late afternoon heading home to their families, we must have appeared to be roadside garbage ourselves, littered across patches of grass where no person would ever think to rest.

It was one week before Christmas. It felt like there

were cauldrons in our chests, ready to boil over. The morning was flat and dull gray and bitterly cold, and as we picked our way along the edge of the road toward the blank billboard at Exit 150 that always marked the end of one segment of cleanup, it began, without warning or fanfare, to snow. Fat, heavy flakes swept around us. We acknowledged this development wordlessly and kept on, crouching to scoop up a brown paper grocery bag or to grasp the long black rubber snake of a blown-out tire. Hot diamonds of snow burned at my cheeks like tears and I rubbed them away before they could melt.

At last we climbed into the back of the van for lunch, and it was then, with the winter's first snow touching softly against the back windows, in the silence created by our disbelief and our madness at the sight of it, that Maurice, face buried in his hands, began to moan a little. He let out a sudden choked sob, and then, to our horror, sat up and began to speak to us, blurry-eyed and disoriented.

"None of y'all prob'ly give a shit about me, I know that," he said, and I looked up at John Jay, expecting him to tell Maurice he was right, but John Jay, and the rest of them, were frozen by his voice. "Last night," he went on, "news came, they got me up outta my bunk." Then he paused and squeezed his eyes tight against some thought. Again, I waited for someone to interrupt him, to tell him he would not be heard; I didn't know what he was working toward but I wanted desperately for him to be quieted. "See, my brother, he ain't mixed up in nothing. Now that's a good kid." Maurice's voice had a shaky, tremulous quality to it. After every few words he took in a deep, staggered breath and then nodded to himself and forged on. "My brother got good marks. My brother worked up at the . . . at the . . . up at Norton Pharmacy in the summertime. My brother, he come an' visit me every week, every Thursday, soon as he get off school. My brother, he run track, too. Carl Lewis, that's what I call him. I say, 'Carl Lewis, you break the school record this week?' I say, 'Carl Lewis, you hittin' the books like I told you?' Kid always had a head on his shoulders. Kid was like a math genius. He ain't ever done dirt, I made him promise me that. I told him, 'Carl Lewis, you ain't even comin' in here like me.' Kid had his shit together. Had himself a nice girl." Maurice teetered to one side like he was about to topple over, then righted himself. He took off his glasses, spit into his right hand, dabbed the thumb of his left hand into the saliva, and worked it in slow, tiny circles at the lenses. We must have watched him for five minutes. My head was clouded. A hot emotion flooded me. I felt the blood push sluggishly through my body. Up front, barely audible, was Greider's country music. A thick white blanket formed over the back windows.

Maurice seemed to have collected himself, but after he had dried his glasses on his pants with numbed difficulty and replaced them over his eyes, he began all at once to cry. "Chaplain come last night an' told me. What happened is, what he says is, what he told me, chaplain said, 'Your brother's dead.'" He wailed at the sound of his own voice presenting the information. "He got done in. Never meant no one no harm, but they done him in on accident, gunnin' for Marquis Eddy next door." Now he was really hysterical, but not a one of us moved or spoke. I was dead inside. Blackness filled me, a bolt of nausea. Something in my core threatened to break apart and I strained to keep it intact. Maurice cried harder, and he kept crying things out. "I can't go see him," he gasped, gripping his head with his baby hands, still sitting straight. "I just want to see him but they puttin' him in the ground. They puttin' him in the ground. They puttin' him underground."

"Shut the fuck up," I heard someone say slowly and evenly, and then I realized the voice was mine. Maurice kept on, and I said it again, a space between each word as though they were four separate commands. "Shut—the—fuck—up!"

But by that point he was beyond us in his misery. He cried on for his brother and for himself. "I want to go home," he wailed. "I want to go home. I want to see my brother. They're puttin' him in the ground. It's snowing. God! It's snowing!" Tears and snot clung to his upper lip.

The van started up at that moment and Greider swung us up onto the road; the back end slid a little in the fresh snow. We drove for three minutes to another spot. Maurice whimpered and struggled for breath. As Greider came around the back of the van to let us out, I shouted at Maurice so loud it shook him from his stupor. "You!" The breath caught in his throat. His eyes came into focus. "Now shut the fuck up," I told him.

What happened next is a little hard to piece together

because it was so unexpected and because it all happened so fast. First the back doors swung open and I saw Greider plainly against the falling snow, a hard, balding man of fifty years, thirty of which he'd spent in Corrections. "Okay, everyone out," he said. He never bore resentment toward any of us as long as we made his job easy and behaved.

The car that hit him seemed to come from nowhere. One moment the road behind Greider was empty, and the next a wide black Buick was flying sideways at all of us. It struck Greider and then the van. The impact tossed us in a heap on the floor. I remember next only that we were all standing outside the van—Colin, Nick, Justin, John Jay, Maurice, and I—and that Greider was crumpled in the snow like a flattened pop can, and that the Buick's tires were spinning like mad on the shoulder. The tires finally grabbed the pavement and the Buick shot away and disappeared into the curtain of whiteness. Already, snow had begun to accumulate over Greider's legs, his back, and his arms.

The six of us stared dumbly at one another. Here it was, a chance for escape. The keys had burrowed a place in the snow a few inches from Greider's hand. We could be miles away before anyone even knew what had happened. But our time at Galloway Lake was nearly half over. Running made no sense. They would catch us again and this time they'd keep us in for longer. In our minds we had only a few months to go and then we would be free.

Had Maurice remained silent, the next part of it might have gone differently. "My glasses," he said to nobody, grop-

ing blindly toward the ground. "Where are my glasses?"
John Jay turned toward him and made this odd sound, a
kind of low and disapproving hum, and launched himself at
Maurice, ramming him with his forearm and shoulder.
Maurice crashed to the earth and lay there stunned for half
a second staring up into the blank sky before John Jay
landed on him, flailing his fists, crying, "Stupid nigger, stupid nigger, stupid nigger." Then all of us were around Maurice, dragging and carrying him to the side of the van, out of
sight of the infrequent passing cars. He never raised a hand
up in defense; he never had the chance. Two of us held
Maurice by his shoulders up against the van while we took
turns battering him. We hit him with our elbows and with
our fists. We kicked at him. We spit on him and shouted
things. All the while the snow fell. Giant snowflakes stuck
in our hair. Maurice's blood was pink on our hands and on
our uniforms; the madness of it brought great wild smiles
to our faces. We danced strange jigs and yelped and sang. It
seemed as if our whole lives had been lived in preparation
for this celebration. We beat Maurice savagely, with pride,
with glory.

After a long, long time, we had expended ourselves. We
stood apart from one another. Maurice lay bloodied and broken, halfway beneath the van. John Jay stared out toward
the bare trees of the birch woods before us. Nick caught
snowflakes on his outstretched palm. Justin watched the
road. Presently, Colin broke away and went over to Greider's
motionless form. "Hey, guys," Colin said vacantly, "he's pretty

bad messed up. We better get him to a hospital." John Jay grunted in agreement and the two of them lifted Greider gently into the back of the van. He was still breathing. John Jay climbed in beside him and tried to comfort him. Nick and Justin joined John Jay. I sorted through the spiny ball of keys for the one to the driver's door, got in up front, and reached over to unlock the far side for Colin. He got in, and then, as an afterthought, we both got out and pulled Maurice from under the van and put him in back with the others. I started the van, crossed the eastbound lanes, bumped over the grassy median, and headed west, toward Jackson and the hospital there, into the snowstorm.

Already, my mind had recoiled from the beating. It occurred to me in my daze, as I leaned forward in the seat, flipped on the lights and the wipers, and fought to keep the van from fishtailing while still driving as quickly as I could, that just a few hours before it had been autumn—late autumn, but not yet winter—and that now it was winter. I became dimly aware that although I would be freed in the spring, it would not be long before I was locked up again, and that realization hurt me worse than anything. I knew also that the only way I could have avoided this future of a lifetime of incarceration was if, immediately after the accident, we had grouped up and gone for help, or if right away we had attempted escape. Escape would have been impossible, but flight would have substituted for what had just transpired—that terrible release—which I could not in that moment, or for many years, remember.

THE LONE SURFER OF MONTANA, KANSAS

WE WERE ON STATE ROAD 400 zooming across yellow Kansas and Sally and I were sore at each other. As my navigator, one of her duties was to call out speed limit signs whenever we flapped our way into each broken-down hamlet, population 104, with its obligatory pair of boarded-up grain-and-feed stores, school, five-and-dime, sad windowless bar, cluster of tin houses that begged for a cyclone—strange old men leaning on shovels in dirt yards—and always, toward the end of the drag, a cop car with its nose peeking out from behind a shuttered Dairy Queen that hadn't served a Blizzard or a dog since 1981. Half an hour before, in a town called McCune, Sally, high off the landscape or lost perhaps in her ragamuffin blues, missed not one but three signs for us to slow down—in descending order, fifty-five, forty-five, and thirty miles per hour, according to the mad and mystified county sheriff who pulled us over and had me clocked at eighty-nine. The sheriff, switching off between aghast disbelief and berserk incoherence, claimed that "the Book" required him to lock me up overnight, but offered to let me off "easy" with a $220 ticket. To her credit, Sally peeped up and explained our navigator arrangement and told the sheriff that it was her fault, she'd been daydreaming and hadn't warned me, but the sheriff merely fixed her with a crude empty stare that implied either a low command of English or cannibalistic urges. Five minutes later, flying south again, the wind sucked the bright orange ticket off the dashboard and out the window. I wasn't going back for it. Really, I could not have cared less about the whole incident—and in truth had kind of gotten off on the old tubby sheriff dude—but the encounter drove Sally deeper into her sadness, and when I told her not to be so hard on herself, that it wasn't no thang, she snapped at me to leave her the hell alone, and we hadn't spoken a word since. Which is why I was so stunned when all of a sudden, as the sun went down and cast the world in red, despairing light and we shot past the same sagging barns and ragged cornfields with trucks up on blocks again and again, Sally seized my arm in great excitement and cried out, "Stop the car, stop the car; Gully, stop the car!"

I lurched off the road in alarm and we did a nice little *Dukes of Hazzard* one-eighty on the slanted gravel shoulder so we were facing back the way we came and staring into our own fantastic cloud of dust. Sally laughed sweetly and gave me a wide-eyed look of thrill and fright. "Sorry," she gulped. "I didn't mean to make you crash us or anything."

"That's okay," I said. "What's the matter?"

"I thought I saw something's all. I wanted to go back and look."

"What'd you think you saw?"

"A boy." She paused. "I can't even explain it."

I pulled back up onto the pavement. "Want to go look?" She nodded vigorously. I asked her where to go.

"Just drive real slow," she said. "He was on the side of that barn."

We crept forward. The sun slipped to the horizon and tinted the entire sky a radioactive shade of pink. In the distance, a single skinny blue cloud hung low like a lost river barge.

"Slow," said Sally, leaning close to see out my window. I kissed her cheek, but she was too concentrated to notice or perhaps still cross with me. For days she'd been distant. "Slower, Gully!" she said. "Drive quiet. He's right around the corner of that barn-thing."

I had no idea what to expect or to look for. A boy with two heads or twelve arms or the tail of a crocodile, a toddler doing a set of bench-presses with a half-ton Chevy pickup, some long-lost brother or cousin of Sally's—none would have surprised me. We ducked into the barn's long shadow and when we finally edged free of it, the sun was so fiery and red and directly in my eyes that I couldn't see a damn thing, but Sally gasped and clutched my leg and breathed one word, "Look!"

My pupils tightened and unwound furiously, trying to

arrive at a workable setting, all to no avail. Then the sun touched the line of scrub oaks at the horizon and in an instant sank out of sight and everything fell into focus in a hurry, silhouettes against a soft rosy backdrop. The kid was close enough to startle me—no more than twenty-five feet from the road—shirtless and shoeless, in just a pair of baggy shorts, half-squatting, half-standing on a plank that rested in a hammock slung between the dead hulls of two enormous tractors. He faced away, toward the sunset's afterglow, arms extended for balance, legs gently straightening, bending, and straightening again, as though culling an odd new martial art. From his build, he looked like he was in his late teens, but since I couldn't see his face, he could have been anywhere from twelve to twenty.

"That's fuckin' unreal," I said to Sally in a half-whisper. With the hush of dusk and the kid's proximity, I was surprised his head didn't whip around at the sound of my voice. We watched him for another minute. He gyrated his hips slightly, rocked his legs a bit. It was such a private act and the kid so clearly believed he was alone that I felt the same tingle of shame and perverse excitement race up my spine as when I was ten years old and I'd watched through a peephole in the wall when my sister took a shower. The kid swayed and shimmied—I was mesmerized and could not look away.

"He's singing," said Sally, and indeed he was; over the engine's eager hum I made out a rising note or two, like sighs at the night's first stars. Sally's hand found mine and I knew all was forgiven from our little speeding-ticket spat. It seemed she was coming around after drifting from me for a while. We began to kiss. I'd never felt so happy to be right where I was. Crickets rang in great numbers across the fields. Night closed in; the air tasted of dew and wheat, motor oil and manure. I pressed my lips to Sally's strawberry-sugar neck and to the soft spot by her ear. The boy kept up his weird dance. The Grand Canyon had maybe one forti-eth the magnificence.

"I don't want to interrupt him," I told Sally. "I just wish I knew what the hell he was doing."

Sally, always one step ahead, it seemed, gave me a look. "Gully, you don't see what he's doing?"

I looked again. "I *see* what he's doing, I just don't get it exactly." Was it prayer? Meditation? His attention was drawn tightly to his own body and the board under him; he didn't seem to notice the purpling sky or the timepiece tick-tick-ticking of our car. "Girl, listen," I said at last, "I ain't got a fucking clue what that's all about." Then everything clat-tered into place in my mind and I knew exactly what the kid was doing; it was so remote and out of context that I'd been blind to it, but once I had it figured out it seemed ridiculous that I hadn't understood right from the start. I cried it out at the same time as Sally: "He's surfing!" In my excitement my left foot slipped off the clutch and the car stalled and jerked forward. The kid whirled his head and shoulders around like he'd been shot at and in that sudden torque lost his balance and tumbled backward wildly from his board. He hit the ground with a cinder-block thump and lay dazed beneath the hammock.

Sally said, "Oh!" and scrambled over me out of the car. She crossed the road, her legs disappeared into the weedy roadside ditch for a moment, and then she was up on the other side, crouching next to the kid. In an instant she leapt up again, waving frantically. "Gulliver!" she wailed in a taut stretched-out tone reserved for true emergencies, "Gully, come quick! He's hurt bad!"

I'D DISCOVERED SALLY eight months before serving Cokes at a roller rink in Newport News, Virginia. She was a tiny, beautiful freckled creature, twenty years old, shy and sad, with big green eyes speckled gray. We'd been traveling together since—a long haul to California to see her sister, then back to the East Coast, a month in D.C., a month in Michigan, down to Pensacola for a couple of months to move my uncle into a home, and after cleaning out his old place, back to Michigan. We both thought it might be nice to pick one spot and settle in for a spell. Sally suggested Arizona. She'd heard it was a mecca for hot-air balloon pilots and she wanted to learn to fly hot-air balloons. So it was decided.

As soon as we packed up the car and got on the road, though, Sally began to fade from me. There had always been times when she'd gotten sad and tuned out for an hour or two, but in the past I'd been able to pull her from the darkness. Now I felt powerless; I even began to wonder if perhaps somehow I was the source of her misery, a suspicion she all but confirmed the morning before at a Waffle House outside Effingham, Illinois, when she told me she was thinking about hopping aboard a Greyhound bus back to Newport News. If she was homesick, I said, I'd be happy to go to Virginia, but she said no, she was thinking about going back *alone*.

This sudden shift of feeling was as mystifying as it was painful. I loved her terribly and I knew she loved me, too. I also knew that she held things back, that she hadn't yet fully revealed herself to me, but I'd figured that's why we were headed to Arizona—to explore each other, to open ourselves completely, to see what shapes love could take down in the desert. Those prospects, apparently, were too frightening for her. She'd been through a lot; for her, closeness was difficult, even harrowing. Still, it seemed to me that if we made it down to Arizona, she'd stick it out and we could start a life together. But if she got too panicked or sad along the way, she'd make me take her to the nearest bus station—Wichita, Oklahoma City, Albuquerque— and that would be it, all would be lost.

For two days my stomach had been freighted with a block of fear and nervousness heavy as a bowling ball. I'd done all I could, though, to play it cool. If I didn't want to lose Sally, I felt my best bet was a) to avoid getting moody and depressed and just try and have fun and be happy, and b) to take all the small two-lane highways I could and plot a route that dodged every city big enough to have a bus station. I explained taking the back roads to Sally by telling her, "You can't see this country from the interstate." Which was also true.

THE KID WAS HURT bad indeed. He blinked up at the sky and trembled a bit, like a penny nail awaiting the blow of a hammer. White bone jutted from his right arm at the elbow. Dark blood pooled in the dirt. "You guys scared the hell outta me," he said. "I didn't see you there." He had his teeth clenched against the pain, but didn't seem to realize the nasty extent of his injury.

"Christ," I said, kneeling down. "Listen, what's your name?"

"Kyle." He tried to raise his arm up to offer his hand but winced and squealed, "God-*damn!*"

"Kyle, listen," I said. "Your arm's broke. You got to go to a hospital." He gave an aww-shucks stage groan like he'd been grounded from a high-school dance. I asked where he lived.

"Right back there, see the house, end of the field?"

"Your parents home?"

"No, no one's there."

"Then you have to come with us." I tore my shirt off and gave it to Sally to wrap around his arm. I asked him where the closest hospital was.

"'S in McCune. Know where that is?"

"I know where that is." I glanced up at the hammock

for the first time and was struck silent with amazement by what I saw—Kyle's board, which from the road I'd taken for a fat length of plywood, was in fact a real-deal full-size surfboard, brand new from the looks of it, Day-Glo orange and yellow with a ghoulish skater motif of full-chested ladies and laughing skulls and the words BIG KAHUNA painted at the tip and the tail. We were something like nine thousand miles from the Pacific. I'd have been less stunned had a troop of elephants burst from the barn.

"Nice board, right?" said Kyle.

"You *surf*?"

"You saw me."

"Jesus! You ever been to the ocean?"

"Nope. But I'm learning now so when I get there I'll already know." Quickly he went on, as though he mistook my astonishment for skepticism. "I've got a videotape and everything," he said. "It's an instructional videotape. It's not just dumb stuff like, *'Be the wave,'* it's got good pointers." He began to sit up and shift his weight around to get a better view of his board but then he howled in agony. "Oh man," he said, digging for his injured arm, starting to cry a little, "I think it's broken. I think it's broken."

Sally and I hauled him to his feet and maneuvered him down to the car, where we loaded him gingerly but hastily into the backseat as if he were a rare piano stool we'd smuggled from the warehouse at an estate auction. "What about my board?" croaked Kyle.

"What about it?"

"We can't just leave it there."

"Why not? You think someone's really gonna mess with it?"

"I don't know. It took me two an' a half years to save for it. We got to take it to the house."

I dashed back up and lifted his board from the hammock. It was unwieldy, nearly ten feet long; I couldn't figure out how to carry it and finally just took it by its tip and dragged it down through the high grass, then at the road heaved it high above my head and jammed it through the open driver's-door window and through, so it stuck out the window on the far side. My shirt, fastened tight around the crook of Kyle's arm, was sopped with blood. He'd begun to turn a bit blue. "Look, we're not stopping at the house," I said. "We'll just take the board with us." Sally hopped in back beside Kyle and tended to him like a sweet nurse, telling him to keep his arm elevated. I leapt behind the wheel, started the beast up, swatted on the headlights, and gunned full-throttle for McCune.

IT SEEMED IMPORTANT to keep Kyle's mind off his injury. If he slipped into shock, extracting directions from him would prove a serious drag. Sally appeared to have the same instincts; she began to pepper him with questions. Kyle answered in single gasps. He said he was fifteen, he was in the ninth grade, his high school was called Benton Consolidated. Sally asked how old she thought we were. "I

don't know," he squeaked. "Eighteen? Twenty-two?" He
kept trying to turn himself to peer out the back window as
though we were on the lam from federal agents. The wind
battered his board up and down against the door frame—
with greater and greater force the faster we went.

"What's your dad's name?" Sally asked him.

"Roger."

"Keep your arm up. What's your mom's?"

"Millie."

I watched them in the rearview. Kyle had a buzz cut
with tails at the ears and in back—the look a Kansas kid
might figure would serve him well on the beaches of Mal-
ibu. He had the high forehead, pronounced cheekbones,
tiny ears, nose and mouth, and weak chin of an old Okie
settler. His family had probably been out west for ten gen-
erations. Over the fireplace mantel back at the house, I
imagined, hung sepia-toned portraits of great-bearded severe-
eyed men with muskets, staring out from the tail end of
wagon trains. I marveled at Kyle's surfboard as it banged and
boogied beside me. What would his ancestors have made of
the BIG KAHUNA? But that was what the world had come
to—with cable TV there was no longer any such thing as ge-
ographical isolation. I'd seen kids in the Arctic Circle sport-
ing Jordan jerseys.

Sally continued her kind interrogation, asking Kyle to
list his friends, the kids on his baseball team by position,
and each of his teachers, but I kept busting in to ask him
questions about surfing. I was blown away by the whole

idea of it. Kyle named his nine favorite surfers; he explained what it meant to ride goofy-footed (which I'd
wondered about for years); he told stories about the monster surf off Oahu and Perth. Every detail brought a wild
smile to my face. Were there kids in Bel Air with a fascina-
tion for farming? Or boys in Bed-Stuy swinging lassos on
fire escapes to train for the rodeo circuit?

It was all too much. The backseat was smeared with
blood, as though we'd had some catastrophe with chain
saws. A strangely troubled and vacant look darkened
Sally's face—I was losing her again. I clamped my foot
down and the white dashboard needle slid past ninety.
Kyle's board yammered on.

"You got brothers or sisters?" I shouted over my shoulder, looking for a new topic of distraction.

"One sister," said Kyle, beginning to fade.

"Yeah? What's her name?"

"Joanie."

"Joanie, huh?" I was hollering like an idiot, but the
more Kyle retreated, the more I felt I had to compensate
in order to keep him conscious. He'd lost a lot of blood.
"So how old's Joanie?"

"Almost four."

"Four, huh? She's probably a pest, right?"

"Look, I don't know if I can really talk about Joanie, okay?"

"Okay," I said, but he'd caught me off-guard. What the
hell was *that* all about? I swung into the opposite lane and
blew by a horse trailer and a pair of old Ford pickups be-

fore an oncoming plow forced me back to the right side. Sally said to watch my speed; I didn't need another ticket, but I figured that most cops would appreciate the circumstances. In the rearview, Kyle's eyes had dimmed to a thirty-watt flicker. "Kyle," I said. No response. "Kyle!" He looked up dreamily. "Kyle, why don't you tell me about your sister, Joanie, all right?"

He sank lower in the seat and closed his eyes. Either it was truly a painful subject for him or he was about to flat-line in the back of my car. Now *that* would be a tricky one to explain if the same county sheriff pulled me over. "Well, sir, I might as well be straight with you—me and the missus here are smuggling dead white kids up to Canada; you wouldn't believe what a lung can fetch on the open market in Montréal. Don't mean to be tearing up the road, but you see, most organs only stay fresh for about twelve hours."

We hit a break in the pavement and Kyle and Sally jolted forward in unison. Kyle's eyelids reared open like twin garage doors and he turned his head slowly right to left, checking out his surroundings with the curiosity and confused indignation of a freshly captured ape coming off tranquilizers on his second day at the Indianapolis Zoo.

"How you doin', champ?" I called over the seat.

He blinked a couple times and said at last, "My surf-board. It can't be good for it to keep hitting against the window like that. Is there a way to roll up the window so it's wedged better, or could you secure it somehow or something? It's just making a god-awful racket back here."

"Yeah, yeah. No problem." I leaned my full weight onto the end of the board and managed for the most part to hold it down. My concern was shifting to Sally, who'd donned a mask of supreme displeasure. Perhaps she was upset about sharing the backseat with our passenger, the one-man blood drive. She hadn't spoken for a few minutes, and I imagined she was outlining all the things she'd do on her first day back in Virginia. I was going to lose her! The thought of it dizzied my insides.

Kyle scooted up in his seat so he was closer to my ear. "You know what cystic fibrosis is?" he asked softly.

"What?"

"What it is, it's a disease," said Kyle. "A genetic birth disease. And my sister Joanie's got it."

"Fuck."

"Yeah, it's a pretty bad disease to have. I think about the worst one. It's painful, I mean *painful*. It's like a war, you against your own body." He cradled his arm, cringed, and sat back a little.

I had an entirely new image in my mind of Kyle's home. Gone were the pictures over the fireplace, the wagon wheel, the antique loom; in their place I saw a metal cot cocooned in slender silvery tubes, stark fluorescent bulbs overhead, boxes of hospital-issue latex gloves and green Ziplocs stacked on counters and tabletops and the arms and seat of every chair, and here and there mysterious tools of hard black rubber. It was never the blindly rich whose families were zapped with this kind of misfortune. Cerebral palsy, spina bifida, muscular dystrophy, cystic fibrosis—all the domain of good honest working folk living on dilapidated farms or in sad run-down subdivisions, mining shacks, trailer parks, public-housing high-rises, or one-room flats over abandoned transmission shops at the edge of town. We veered around another couple of trucks. Kyle's surfboard flailed beneath me. The night seemed mournful and ominous.

"Kyle," I said, "isn't your sister's birthday coming up?"

"What?"

"You said she was almost four."

"Yeah, but she's supposed to die this week."

"This week?" said Sally. "What do you mean?"

"She's not gonna make it. My dad called and told me. It'll probably be tomorrow or the next day, the weekend at the latest. She's kind of a fighter."

This news had Sally upset. "Where is she? Is she at home?"

"No, she's at the hospital. Same place we're heading. My mom and dad are up there, too." His words circulated heavily around the car's whooshing interior like tin butterflies on a mobile made in shop class at a state penitentiary.

"I'm sorry," I told him. In the mirror our gazes met.

"'S'okay," Kyle said, but all at once he sputtered and his face broke and he began to really cry. He turned away as though shamed by his tears. Sally moved close, held him in a half hug, and tried to soothe him. Kyle only ducked farther away. His shoulders shook, his chest heaved. He whimpered and struggled for breath.

Sally refused to let him suffer alone—she put both arms around him and shushed him and told him everything would be all right. A tingling roller-coaster rush swept up from my groin to my stomach as I had a little front-seat revelation that Sally was truly an angel on this Earth. My love for her doubled and redoubled.

Then suddenly Kyle whirled on Sally and me with a wild look. His face was teary and pink. He waved his broken wing high and I felt two drops of blood from the red-soaked shirt spatter the back of my neck. "I know why this happened to me!" he screeched. "I'll tell you why this happened. It's a punishment, that's what. It's Joanie punishing me. Or God!"

"Kyle, no," I said sharply. "God's not like that. He's not vindictive, dog. God's all about love, not punishment. It's not your fault, anyways! You did all you could do. You showed your sister love."

"No, I didn't!" he cried. Now he was really hysterical. Sally tried in vain to restrain him. "It *is* my fault," he said. "It *is* my fault! You don't understand—I wished she was dead! Every night, I wished she was dead." He slumped over in the seat, racked with sobs, caught in a devastating pain.

In the middle of the road an orange paper scrap flashed in the headlights then disappeared under the car—it was my speeding ticket, I realized, which signaled that we were getting close to McCune. I kept my toe to the floor. If the authorities out here didn't want drag races they shouldn't have made every state road in Kansas so goddamn straight. There hadn't been one curve all the way from Kyle's house. A fireplace log placed on the gas pedal could pilot its way to Wichita.

In the back Kyle poured his heart out to Sally but through his tears I could only make out a little of what he said. Every third night he'd had to stay awake with his sister and scrape mucus from her throat at five-minute intervals. He'd had to scoop it out with his fingers. God, he wailed, how he'd hated it! Finally, in the midst of describing the glop, he broke down completely and could not go on. At my side his surfboard wrestled violently for freedom like an orca caught in a trawler's net. "In a minute, Kyle," I said, glancing back at him, "I'm gonna need to know what turns to take to get us to the hospital." A half-second later I saw the sheriff's car in a dark weedy lot up ahead and by the time I pounded the brake and looked down to check our speed we were flying past him at a hundred and two.

THE COP SPRANG AFTER US, red-and-blues twirling giddily. We had enough of a lead, I figured maybe we could just outrace him. When I jammed my foot back to the accelerator, though, Sally sensed my chain of thought and reproached me. "Gulliver! What are you doing?" I realized she was right, of course, no sense compounding the situation and getting Rodney Kinged. Besides, with Kyle in his current state, we'd need help finding the ER.

I coasted up a long incline and jagged into a tiny paved lot glowing with blue light from the town's lone street-lamp. The little trailer-sized milk-and-cigs convenience store parked before us looked closed, but a neon OPEN sign blazed pink inside a Plexiglas porthole near the door. A pair of rusted gas pumps looked on from the shadows like old gossiping fishermen. In the back of the car, Kyle poked his head high to see what was going on. The sheriff rolled up cautiously and pinned us in. His sirens carouseled in silent red-blue trifectas. I climbed from the car. "This'll just take a minute."

It was the same cop who'd pulled us over an hour before. He was rattling a mile a minute into his radio, and when he saw me coming toward him, bare-chested and splotched with blood, he drew his pistol and leveled it at me out his window. "Just stay where you are, boy," he said. I wasn't going to mess around with this particular deputy while I was staring down the barrel. It was clear he'd been itching to fire the thing for years and was aware that this might be his best chance before retirement. Through a series of careful negotiations, switching the gun back and forth from one hand to the other, he managed to wriggle free of his seat belt and lug himself out of the car without ever allowing his aim to waver from my chest. We faced each other at twelve feet. Oh, he was a mean-looking sonofabitch. Earlier, for some reason, he'd seemed less imposing. Cops always take it personal when you crack a hundred on their turf.

The sheriff clicked his jaw and sized me up. "You look awful familiar," he said at last. "And it's funny. I never figured on seeing you again."

"Honestly," I replied, "I felt the same way. But there's a kid bleeding to death in the back of my car and we're trying to get him to the hospital, so I was thinking maybe we could just go to the hospital and then you and I can figure everything else out once we get there."

He chuckled. "Oh, I don't think so. I think we'll wait right here until *Fred* arrives." He invoked the name with a dark smile, as though he'd radioed for backup from Beelzebub himself. As if in response, a siren whoop-*whoop*ed somewhere in the night. The sheriff nodded, relaxed and in his groove now, his revolver extended with both hands. He was enjoying things a tad too much.

"Dude, you got to listen," I said. "I'm not fucking around. Just go over and look in my car. Just go and look! The kid broke his arm. It's bad. The bone's sticking out. He's in shock and it's got to get treated, I'm serious."

"Once Fred gets here we'll sort things out." He stole a quarter-second glance toward Sally and Kyle. "What do you got in the front seat there?" he asked.

I looked over. "Oh, that? It's a surfboard, sir. The BIG KAHUNA."

He nodded like it all made sense and further incriminated me in his mind. I turned to Sally and Kyle and gave them a little yeah-he's-got-his-gun-out-but-everything's-cool flip of my hand. The two of them, in the backseat of my car, blank faces swirling with red and blue, looked like a pair of frightened third-graders who'd been apprehended for poisoning their gym teacher and were awaiting transport to the precinct jail. Kyle, perhaps misinterpreting my little wave, or just disoriented from his fucked-up arm and his grief, slid across the seat and pushed open the door on the far side and started to climb out. Sally dove after him and grabbed him around the neck and shoulders but Kyle shrugged free. The sheriff swung himself ninety degrees so his gun was on Kyle. He barked, "Hey, get back in the car!"

Kyle eyed him with the sullen confusion of a patient at a home for the disturbed who's stumbled upon two orderlies screwing in the broom closet. He made his way around the back of the car toward the sheriff, holding his broken arm straight out ahead of him. My blood-soaked shirt dangled off like a black sea lamprey. The sheriff shouted at him again and retreated a couple steps behind the shield of his open door. He swung the gun back toward me for a second, as though to discourage a charge, then aimed back at Kyle. Faced with a second shirtless kid covered with blood, the sheriff paled and worked his jaw furiously, as though trying to piece together what kind of gruesome act he might have nabbed us speeding away from. Again, unsteady and fearful now, he told Kyle to freeze, but all Kyle wanted to do was show him his arm—slack-eyed and dull-faced he waddled closer. The sheriff looked at me, frantic, "Tell him to stop! I'll blow him away!" Except his weapon was pointed at me not at Kyle. He had the trigger squeezed back, I guessed, about two-thirds of the way. It amazed me how quickly things could get out of hand once a gun entered the picture. Getting plugged by a cop would be no great surprise, but I'd have never laid a wager down on dying in Kansas.

The next part unraveled in wild succession—from the car, Sally let out a piercing scream; at the same moment, a plain-looking blond lady banged her way out of the convenience store hugging four two-liters of Dr Pepper. The sheriff spun—the tip of his revolver flashed—and the lady in the doorway howled and flipped backward into the store. A fraction of a second later the sound of the gunshot rocked the night.

The sheriff, standing in a cloud of white smoke, slowly lowered his gun. Sally fought with her door but couldn't seem to work the handle. Kyle turned toward me, suddenly lucid, a goofy smile lighting his face. "Holy shit!" he cried. Up and down State Road 400, farm dogs began to yap and croon as the explosion reverberated from house to house, across field after field.

A CAR'S ENGINE THRUMMED powerfully over the crest of the hill and immediately a second cruiser appeared, its headlights punching the dark, one-two, one-two. The cop bumped his ride into the lot and jumped out—a young, huge, athletic marine type, head shaved bald—Fred, I presumed. His voice was high and squeaky, a poor match for his frame. "Hey, is that *you*, Kyle?" he said. "I was just headed out to your house. Your dad asked me to run out and get you." Then he paused. "Jesus Christ, what the hell'd you do to yourself?"

The sheriff broke in. "Fred, we've got a bystander down. Inside there." He nodded toward the market. "Listen, I'll call an ambulance, you want to go check on 'em?"

Fred asked a few questions and somehow the sheriff, without explaining what had happened, got it across that any danger there had been when he'd radioed for help had passed, and that there were no suspects lurking in the store, just a woman who'd been shot. Kyle and Sally and I followed right behind Fred as he hurried over to the door and yanked it open.

A tiny, bent, hundred-and-ten-year-old codger greeted us, plastic mop wielded high over his head in an impotent pose of protection and threat. "Mr. Morton, slow down," said Fred, "it's just me." He plucked the mop from the old-timer's hands. A few feet beyond, on her belly under a rack of candy and wiper fluid, the woman the sheriff had cut down yodeled and wheezed and sniffled to herself, doused in blood and soda. The bullet had caught her in the hip. Fred rolled her over. "Miss—listen—you're gonna be all right. All right? Do you hear me? You're fine; you're just fine." He reminded me of myself a half hour earlier with Kyle. "Miss," he said, "tell me your name."

"Glenda," she wailed.

"Where are you from, Glenda?"

"Mutt—Mutt—Mutton Springs, Missou-rah."

"What'cha doing in McCune?"

"Visiting my sister, Nancy Mullaney."

"Nancy Mullaney? What a woman." He went on, and as he talked he hastily examined her, tore a handkerchief from his pocket, pressed it to the wound, and strapped it on tightly with three six-foot strands of red licorice from the rack beside him. He was every bit as sharp and competent as the sheriff outside was a quack and a goon. "Okay, now, Glenda, here's what we're gonna do. We're gonna stand you up and get you out to my car. Can you stand?" He turned and gave me a slight nod that meant he'd identified me as the most capable assistant. I went over to them, and Fred and I struggled with the woman for a moment but couldn't get her off the floor.

I had an idea. "Wait here for ten seconds," I said. I dashed out to my car to grab the BIG KAHUNA. The sheriff was on his CB again, begging miserably for an EMT crew. He watched, baffled, as I tugged Kyle's surfboard out my passenger-side window and headed back inside.

"Good," said Fred. "Perfect."

We rolled Glenda onto the board. Sally and I raised the back end up, Fred lifted the front, Old Man Morton held the door open, and we made our way out to the parking lot. Kyle buzzed near, terribly dismayed. "She's too heavy for the thing, I'm telling you. It's not built for that. It's gonna snap right in two!"

The sheriff about fainted with relief when he saw that

Glenda was breathing and alert. "St. Mary's on its way," he said.

Fred shook him off. "Forget the ambulance. We'll take her there ourselves. Save ten minutes, easy." Sally opened his rear door, I dropped my end down on the seat, and Fred tilted his end high. Glenda slid in. She was in obvious pain but had no idea what had happened to her. She probably thought her appendix had burst.

Fred handed me the surfboard and hustled around to his door. I told him I was going to follow him—I had Kyle with me and he was hurt, too.

"Okay," said Fred, hopping in, revving up his RPMs, and toggling the siren. "Can you drive fast?"

THE HOSPITAL WAS CALLED St. Mary's of Lesterton and McCune. It consisted of two small, squat, shabby brick buildings, one beside the other, connected by a yellow loading dock. A bedraggled American flag propped out front gave the place the look of a converted V.F.W. bingo hall. I hoped some old Korean War infantrymen still kept a game going in the basement; it wasn't too likely that the ER staff had much experience removing Colt rounds.

Fred parked beside the dock, I swung in next to him, and the sheriff pulled up behind us. Everyone piled out. We loaded Glenda onto the surfboard again, carried her inside, down a long hallway, and into a dismal twelve-by-ten waiting room with a few empty chairs, stacks of beat-up magazines on side tables, and, mounted high in one corner, a TV flickering cartoons. The sheriff furiously pounded a bell at the front counter while the rest of us stood there covered in blood, looking around at one another. Two prim gray-haired nurses emerged from a room in back and gasped at the carnage. One got on the PA and hissed for urgent assistance. "The sheriff's here with his accident victim. Victims." The other nurse seized Sally and began pulling her off toward triage. Sally protested that she wasn't hurt. "Don't worry, pretty thing," said the nurse. "They'll get you stitched up, you'll be fine."

Eventually the doctors arrived and sorted everything out. They gauged Glenda's injury the most serious and wheeled her away. Kyle got a heavy gauze wrap, four enormous blue painkillers, and a cot in the hallway. "This'd be rad to surf on," he said. "Gulliver, roll me down to that door. Come on!" I said no, but agreed to take his surfboard into the bathroom and rinse off Glenda's blood. I figured I'd clean myself up, too. Sally came along.

Washing up, we were alone for the first time since we'd first seen Kyle. Sally started to cry. The evening had taken its toll. "Oh Gull," she said, "I don't know. I can't help but feel like we caused all this." I pulled off her shirt and scrubbed her down with wet paper towels. Forlorn tears made a beeline for her chin. "What were we doing in the first place, sitting there spying on him like that?" Her voice was tremulous. "It's always bad news, soon's we get off the interstate. Why'd we even get off? Was it your idea or mine?"

"It was mine," I said. "But look, love, nothing's our fault. We didn't shoot anyone; we didn't push Kyle off his board. You heard the kid. He had ill will toward his sister. God punished him. He had it coming."

She slugged me. "You're a prick! You think you're so funny. You know, that cop could have shot *you* just as easy. You don't even value your own life, why should I expect you to value anyone else's?" She snatched her shirt from me, fought with it a moment to find the neck hole, then plunged it on over her head and stomped out.

I tagged after her, dragging the surfboard. "You're right, Sally, I'm sorry. I was just fucking around; that's how I deal with shit. My bad, all right?"

She pouted on and wouldn't talk to me. First bus to Newport News, she was good as gone.

The sheriff had pulled a chair out into the hallway and sat across from Kyle, thumbing through the pages of a tattered *Ranger Rick* without reading it. Since the gunplay, he'd shed every bit of his cockiness and bite, and now, still badly shaken, he reminded me of an NFL coach fired four games into the season, trying not to weep at his press conference. Usually I'd find great joy in seeing someone brought down by their own idiocy—especially a cop—but the sheriff's hot, billowing self-hatred was almost too much to bear. I could picture him later that night going for a long drive, oldies station cranked at full volume, two bewildered hounds on the seat beside him, pulling off the road by the creek where he'd first made love to his high-school girlfriend, fighting his way down to the water, tearfully kneeling down and blowing his brains out on the weedy bank.

"What happened to Fred?" I asked him.

"Someone got the Luskovich's cat with an arrow. Fred went to check it out." He went back to his magazine.

Sally stood examining something on Kyle's good arm. I went over to look and she glowered at me. On his twiggy bicep, Kyle had a tiny eyeball-sized tattoo of a baseball, and over it, in a curved brow, the word MONTANA.

I said, "You're from Montana?"

"Montana's a town," he replied. "That's where we live. We all got tattoos, my whole team." The pills had him woozy. He laid back and rubbed his eyes and his cheeks. I asked if he'd seen his parents yet, if they knew what had happened. He said the nurse had told them, but something was happening with Joanie; they'd be up to see him as soon as they could. "No matter what," he said, "don't tell 'em how it happened. They didn't even want me to get my board. I'm not gonna give 'em an excuse to take it away." Then he grew concerned. "Hey, can you make sure my board ends up in my dad's van? Would you mind, one of you, making sure you get it to him?"

Sally and I looked at each other. Already her venom had faded. With her eyes she asked me, You want to go? "Okay," I said.

"Let's go take care of it," said the sheriff, rising, tucking the magazine under his arm.

I hoisted the BIG KAHUNA onto my shoulder. Once Kyle

saw that his surfboard was headed to safety, he closed his eyes and was instantly asleep, dreaming of the swells on Puget Sound or Nantucket, I imagined. We all watched him breathe for a minute. Then the nurse returned and wheeled him away to get worked on. Sally took the sheriff's seat and said she'd wait there, and I followed the sheriff down the hall. At the end of it, I heard little footsteps pattering up from behind, but the board kept me from turning my head. Sally bobbed up at my side, a strange scared look on her face. I thought she'd decided to get a Greyhound ticket home. She peered at me sideways for a long beat and a half—my heart flimflammed—then she leaned up on her tippy-toes, planted a quick teeny kiss on my cheek, and darted away. "Come on, I got you," said the sheriff, holding the door for me.

"Thanks." I walked through, the gladdest man on Earth.

OFF A QUIET BASEMENT CORRIDOR, in a dim nook gloomy with streamers and half-deflated helium balloons, a man and woman sat on either side of a small hospital bed that held a tiny girl wrapped in sheets. Their faces looked beaten. The man sagged in his chair, weary and defeated, while the woman sat forward, tense, wringing a black cloth between her hands. The sheriff paused at the entrance door. "Roger. Millie."

The man looked up slowly and acknowledged him with a nod. "Randy."

The sheriff crowded in; I left the surfboard out in the hallway and followed behind him. He introduced me. "This here's the boy who found Kyle and brought him in."

Kyle's father looked at my chest, operating in a haze of loss and sorrow. "Thank you," he said softly.

"Yeah." It hurt to see a dude in such pain.

"How's Kyle doing?" he asked.

"Kyle's fine," I said. "He just went into surgery. He really messed himself up pretty bad but he'll be okay."

"Good. Okay." His gaze returned to his daughter, and the sheriff and I immediately slipped from his awareness. Little Joanie's eyes were closed tightly, her face scrunched up in an expression of fierce concentration. With each shallow breath her covers rose and fell. I was surprised to see that she wasn't hooked in to any machines—not even a heart monitor or an IV drip. On a shelf beside her bed, two miniature toy soldiers, like the ones in *The Nutcracker*, hovered at rigid attention. Their blank faces and empty blue eyes gave them an odd haunting presence. The crazed notion came into my head that somehow they were responsible for the girl's sickness, and that if we could get them away from her, her health would steadily return.

Joanie coughed weakly. A dark drop of blood appeared at the corner of her mouth and her mother lunged forward with the black cloth to wipe it away, then coiled back into her chair. She was full of manic vigilance; her husband was resigned and absent. I wondered how long they'd maintained these positions at Joanie's bedside. Days? Weeks?

Months? The room was thick with accumulated grief. I felt the great weight of all tragedies where a child dies and their parents have to suffer through—leukemia and its cycle of chemo, remission, and relapse, a drowning off Martha's Vineyard, a kid struck by a train or caught in the cross fire of two warring gangs. I'd been to some of those funerals. I'd seen the families in the months and years that followed. The pain never seemed to ease.

Beside me, the sheriff cleared his throat. "Roger." Kyle's father didn't seem to hear. The sheriff said his name again; this time the dad looked up, fogged, glassy, and greeted the sheriff as though we'd just walked in. Johnny Carson could have paid a visit and a minute later Kyle's pops wouldn't have remembered it. He was absolutely numb. The sheriff introduced me again and explained that we had Kyle's surfboard and that Kyle wanted to make sure it got out to their van. "Why don't you borrow me your keys for a minute," he said. "We'll take care of it."

Kyle's father patted his pockets down and stared about the room. Then he seemed to forget what he was looking for, and he looked back up at us, confused.

"Is your van locked?" said the sheriff. "Maybe it's open, huh? That's it parked right out front, ain't it, big brown Econoline?"

"That's our van," he said. "Is it parked funny? Need me to move it?"

"No, it's fine. We're just gonna go out and put Kyle's surfboard in there."

"You've got Kyle's surfboard? Wait. Oh. It's locked. I'll come with you. There's a trick to it, the back's hard to open." Kyle's father stood and rested his hand for a moment on his wife's shoulder, either to balance himself or in a gesture of solidarity. He brushed past the sheriff and me and lifted a full hoop of keys off a hook by the doorway that held medical charts like it was his key hook at home, then ambled out into the hall. The sheriff and I followed after him.

By silent agreement Kyle's dad took one end of the surfboard and I took the other. The sheriff led us down a narrow passageway and through two sets of double doors, then turned to his left and held open a heavy green door that might have once served as a fire escape, and waited for us to go past. Kyle's dad and I negotiated our way through, up a half-flight of rusty metal steps to a tight landing, and up another half-flight and through one last door into the cool night. We were in a dirt-packed field behind the hospital. Wind kicked grass and paper clutter against the brick.

In my hands, Kyle's surfboard seemed to tingle with a strange electrical current, as though conducting a charge of pain and blistering sorrow from Kyle's dad. We walked in a procession around the side of the building. The sheriff puffed a brief little monologue—more for his own benefit than ours, it seemed—about how the world needed to be more forgiving of itself and how people had to let go of their shortcomings and the things they didn't have and find greater appreciation for the things they did have.

Apparently his brush with manslaughter had him ripe for epiphany. But he was also making an attempt, in his own clumsy way, to bring comfort to Kyle's father, and I couldn't help but be touched. I imagined that from time to time his duties as sheriff required a show of compassion—whenever a lightning strike set someone's house ablaze or a flood ruined someone's crops or a beloved tractor finally broke down for good. Still, I could hardly believe this was the same man who just a couple hours before had been purple with fury over a traffic violation and ready to lynch me.

As we came around the last corner and Kyle's dad's van appeared, parked beside a pair of black Dumpsters, a shiny Ford pickup reared off the main road into the lot and a woman catapulted from the driver's seat and dashed inside.

Kyle's dad spoke for the first time since leaving Joanie's chamber, "Hey, ain't that Nancy Mullaney? I wonder what she's doing here—and in such a hurry!"

The sheriff grunted ambiguously. He wasn't ready to confess the night's full misadventures to Kyle's dad; at the same time he wasn't about to ease off the self-condemnation for pumping lead into an innocent Missourian. With a look of broken remorse, he peered up at the faded Stars and Stripes snapping smartly in the breeze off the hospital's front awning as though the flag itself somehow represented all of his life's failures. Perhaps, I mused, some slight physical handicap had disqualified him from 'Nam—poor vision in one eye, say, or a five-eighths of an inch discrepancy between leg lengths. In all likelihood the sheriff's father had been a paratrooper in France—but the most *he* could ever be was a small-town cop.

Kyle's father gave up his end of the surfboard to undo the back doors of the van. Methodically, still detached from his surroundings, he fiddled with key after key, but couldn't find the right one. His movements seemed drugged. Even if he had the right key, I didn't think he'd be able to get the van open. "Here, let me try," I said. I passed him the board.

The wind picked up, confused which direction to blow. Dark roiling clouds gathered overhead. A powerful storm was on its way. The sheriff glanced this way and that, growing apprehensive and impatient, but I couldn't get the damn van open either. A sweet road-kill odor gusted from the Dumpsters.

The sheriff shouldered me aside and in a second he'd solved the lock. Kyle's dad climbed in to rearrange the tools and fishing gear inside; the sheriff and I passed him Kyle's board. Once the BIG KAHUNA was securely in place, he turned, sat down with his legs hanging over the fender, and buried his head in his hands and began to cry, softly at first, then with rising intensity. I hopped up beside him. The sheriff stepped in close and took us each by the shoulder. The wind forced the van doors inward, sealing our little three-man huddle. Rain thundered off the roof in a five-second burst and drummed away to silence across the lot.

I had a sudden bleak revelation—Kyle would never get

to the ocean. As simple and obvious a notion as it was, it hit me like a gut punch and triggered a terrible, low-sinking chain reaction. My heart grew hard, my insides seized up. Everything seemed hopeless, orphaned, and sad. I felt like everyone on the planet was stuck with their feet in cement, dreaming lonely impossible dreams, wishing on 747s they took for stars. An image tumbled up into my mind of the kid who had shot the Luskovich's cat with an arrow; now, I imagined, he was in his basement, blotting out his emotions watching an old black-and-white Western on an eleven-inch TV while upstairs his parents screamed at each other in the kitchen. I thought of the young, pretty truck-stop waitress, seven-months pregnant, who'd served Sally and me the night before outside Dubuque, and the lawyer in Chicago who'd tagged my bumper at a light, cell phones clamped to both ears like an actor in a parody of modern life. I thought of all the inmates at every sad state facility Sally and I had passed since leaving Virginia—I pictured them at barred windows, looking out across the yard as a storm whirled in with strange green skies then departed, leaving the grass with a wet lustrous shine and a dozen or so puddles on the cement walks. The world had never seemed so beautiful and devastating, so ordinary and broken-down—all of it filled with the same mournful gleam. I felt I'd been everywhere and seen everything and met everyone and that still I knew nothing.

Kyle's dad cried on, neither gaining nor losing momentum. It was the kind of slow interminable release that had no tidy end. His hands covered his face; tears sliced down his chin and popped off his wrists. "'S'okay," said the sheriff. "Oh, Roger, it's okay, it's okay, it's okay." The sheriff's eyes were closed, too, his head tilted back—he was lost in his own throes of pain and melancholy. One of the van doors blew open and I saw a pizza box sail across the road—no flips or spins—just a smooth steady ascent like a magic carpet on takeoff. I imagined it might fly forever, but a moment later it banked off a telephone pole and crashed down.

Kyle's dad sat up straight and pulled his hands from his face. He had a look of serene wonder. I followed his gaze to the sad old flag swishing tirelessly from its roost. I felt like he, the sheriff, and I were the last Americans alive after a great cataclysm, and that we were on a raft at sea, lost and uncertain, drifting toward vast, uncharted lands, unsure who, if anyone, we would find. Kyle's dad, in a low voice, began to sing, slowly, wrenchingly, "A-maz-ing Grace . . . how sweet . . . the sound . . . that saved . . . a wretch . . . like me . . ." The beauty of it was excruciating. The sheriff and I joined in, and the three of us offered ourselves up to the sad Kansas night. "I once . . . was lost . . . but now . . . I'm found . . . was blind . . . but now . . . I see . . ."

HOW I GOT HERE

THEY TOLD US *TO WRITE HOW WE GOT HERE. HOW DID I GET HERE. WHAT DOES THAT MEAN. I GOT HERE IN A BROWN VAN WITH 1 OTHER GUY AND 2 GUYS DRIVING. THEY WERE OK. THEY STOPPED AT A DRIVE-THRU AND GOT US WHOPPERS AND COKES. IN FEDERAL YOU DONT GET COKE, YOU DONT GET SHIT. OUR LAST COKES FOR 4 YEARS. THE GUYS UP FRONT THOUGHT IT WAS FUNNY. REALLY THEY WERE FUCKING DICKS. THEY SAID NOT TO PUT CUSS WORDS IN THESE PROJECTS FOR CLASS BECAUSE OTHER WORDS SAY IT BETTER BUT IM SORRY THOSE GUYS WERE FUCKING DICKS!!!!!!!!!!*

HOW DID I GET HERE. I HIT A DUDE WITH A SHOVEL. THAT WAS A CHARGE OF MALICIOUS WOUNDING. YOU DONT GET FEDERAL FOR MALICIOUS WOUNDING BUT I HAD A NARCOTICS POSSESSION WITH INTENT TO DIS-TRIBUTE THAT I HAD A SUSPENDED SENTENCE FROM AND THE MALICIOUS WOUNDING CHARGE MEANS I HAVE TO SERVE THE NARCOTICS. AFTER FEDERAL I HAVE 4 YEARS IN STATE. STATE AND FEDERAL ARE A LOT

DIFFERENT. STATE YOU GET REC TIME. YOU GET OUT-
DOOR REC AND YOU GOT WEIGHTS. STATE YOU GET A
LOT MORE VISITS. STATE YOU GET COMMISSARY. WELL
FEDERALS GOT COMMISSARY BUT IT SUCKS PLUS YOU
DONT GET COMMISSARY WHEN YOURE IN SOLITARY
AND YOU GET SOLITARY FOR BULLSHIT. LAST WEEK I
SAW A MEXICAN KID GET SOLITARY FOR THE WORST
BULLSHIT EVER. ONE OF THE LUNCH C.O.S SAID THE
KID MUTTERED SOMETHING WHEN HE WALKED PAST
HIM. HE SAID TO THE KID WHAT DID YOU SAY. THE KID
DIDNT EVEN KNOW ENGLISH. HE SAID WHAT I DONT
UNDERSTAND. THE C.O. STARTED YELLING AT HIM AND
THEY GAVE HIM 30 DAYS SOLITARY. BULLSHIT BULL-
SHIT. SORRY FOR THE CUSS WORDS BUT I WAS RIGHT
THERE AND I KNOW THE KID DIDNT SAY ANYTHING.
BUT THATS HOW IT IS!!!!!!!!!!!

HOW DID I GET HERE. MAYBE THEY MEAN HOW
DID I GET HERE TO THE CLASS. KIRBY TOLD ME ABOUT
IT. IM SICK OF TV AND I WANT TO LEARN BETTER WRIT-
ING SO I CAN WRITE GOOD LETTERS TO MISSY AND JE-
NINE. THATS MY SISTER AND MY LITTLE GIRL. BESIDES
KIRBY SAID SOMETIMES CUTE GIRLS COME FROM S.I.U.
TO TEACH CLASS. DAMN WE HAVE THREE TEACHERS
ALL GUYS!!!!!!!!! BUT YOU GUYS ARE OK.

HOW DID I GET HERE. HERE ON THIS PLANET
THEY CALL EARTH. MY MOTHER GOT ME HERE. WELL
I GUESS MY DAD HAD SOMETHING TO DO WITH IT.
NOT MUCH REALLY. MY MOTHERS NAME WAS MAE

LIKE MAE WEST THE MOVIE STAR MISSY ALWAYS SAYS. MY DADS NAME WAS WILLIAM LIKE ME BUT THEY CALLED HIM BILL AND IM WILLIE. MY MOTHER WAS A TALL WOMAN WITH GREEN EYES THEY SAY ALL THE GUYS WERE IN LOVE WITH HER. SHE WAS A WAITRESS AT THE PINTO DINER AT LIVERNOIS AND GRAND. SHE DIED IN A ACCIDENT. A CAR RAN A LIGHT AND HIT HER. THAT WAS IN BATTLE CREEK. I WAS BORN IN DE-TROIT. MY MOTHER WAS 30 WHEN I WAS BORN. RIGHT AFTER I WAS BORN SHE DIED. I WAS LUCKY BECAUSE THE WEEK BEFORE I WAS INSIDE HER STOMACH. BUT I WAS UNLUCKY BECAUSE SHE DIED!!!!!!!!!

I NEVER MET MY DAD BUT I HEARD HE WAS A BAD DUDE. HES IN STATE PRISON IN TENNESSEE RIGHT NOW THATS WHAT I HEARD. HES ABOUT 60 YEARS OLD I THINK. NO WAY IM GOING TO BE LOCKED UP WHEN IM 60. FUCK THAT!!!!!!!!

HOW DID I GET HERE. I WAS STUPID AND I MADE STUPID MISTAKES. I TOOK FREEDOM FOR GRANTED. THAT WAS STUPID BECAUSE WHEN YOU ARE FREE EVEN IF YOU DONT HAVE A CENT TO YOUR NAME EVEN IF YOU HAVE A ASSHOLE AS A BOSS EVEN IF YOU DONT HAVE A JOB AT ALL EVEN IF YOU HAVE A WOMAN WHO RUNS AROUND EVEN IF YOU DONT HAVE A WOMAN AT ALL AND EVEN IF YOUR TRUCK DIES AND YOU HAVE TO ALWAYS TAKE THE BUS OR WALK WELL EVEN IF YOU DON'T HAVE A DAMN THING AT ALL YOU STILL HAVE FREEDOM AND THATS A LOT!!!!!!!!!!

HOW DID I GET HERE. THE JUDGE DIDNT LIKE ME MUCH. HE SAID I WAS A FUCKUP AND A MENACE TO SOCIETY. HE REALLY SAID THAT. THAT WAS IN COURT IN FRONT OF MISSY AND JENINE. HE DIDNT HAVE TO SAY THAT. HE COULD SAY MENACE TO SOCIETY BE-CAUSE I DONT THINK JENINE KNOWS WHAT THAT MEANS BUT HE DIDNT HAVE TO SAY FUCKUP NOT WITH HER RIGHT THERE. THATS HER DADDY HES TALKING ABOUT AND IF I COULD OF I WOULD OF BEAT THE HELL OUT OF HIM. THEY THINK THEY KNOW EVERYTHING BUT THE TRUTH IS THEY DONT KNOW ANYTHING!!!!!!!! ID LIKE TO SEE THAT JUDGE SPEND 1 MONTH IN HERE THEN SEE IF HE KEEPS GIV-ING MAXIMUMS. SOMETIMES I SEE ON TV THAT A JUDGE GETS PUT IN JAIL. I WOULD LIKE IT IF THEY HAD TO COME DOWN HERE TO MARION. NOT SO I COULD BEAT THE HELL OUT OF THEM BUT JUST SO I COULD TALK TO THEM. I WOULD ASK THEM WHY THEY THINK PEOPLE DONT MATTER WHY DONT THEY CARE WHY DONT THEY THINK PEOPLE CAN CHANGE AND WHY THEY CALL SOMEONE A FUCKUP WHEN THEIR LITTLE GIRL IS THERE WATCHING. HOW CAN THEY SAY FUCKUP IN A COURTROOM. WHAT WILL THAT GIRL THINK OF HER DADDY WHEN THE JUDGE SAYS THAT AND THE JUDGE IS ALL FANCY AND SMART IN HIS ROBES AND SUPPOSED TO KNOW EVERYTHING. ILL TELL YOU WHAT. THAT LITTLE GIRL SHELL THINK HER DADDYS A FUCKUP THATS WHAT.

HOW DID I GET HERE. HOW DID I GET HERE. I WISH I KNEW!!!!!!!!!

NOW I AM GOING *TO WRITE ABOUT THE 2 MOST IMPORTANT PEOPLE IN MY LIFE. KIRBY SAID THAT WAS A PROJECT FROM LAST MONTH BEFORE I WAS IN THE CLASS. I AM GOING TO WRITE ABOUT MY LITTLE GIRL JENINE AND MY SISTER MISSY. THEY ARE THE 2 MOST IMPORTANT PEOPLE IN MY LIFE!!!!!!!!!*

MY LITTLE GIRL IS NAMED JENINE. SHE IS 5 YEARS OLD. SHE IS IN THE FIRST GRADE. SHE HAS BLOND HAIR AND GREEN EYES SAME AS HER DADDY. SHE HAS SOME FRECKLES. HER FAVORITE COLOR IS GREEN. HER FAVORITE NUMBER IS 5 BECAUSE THATS HOW OLD SHE IS. LAST YEAR HER FAVORITE NUMBER WAS 4. IT WAS 3 BEFORE THAT AND BEFORE THAT I DONT THINK SHE KNEW WHAT A NUMBER WAS. HER FAVORITE FOOD IS JELLY BEANS GREEN ONES. SHE DOESNT LIKE ICE CREAM BECAUSE ITS TOO COLD.

I REMEMBER ALL THE FUN THINGS WE USED TO DO TOGETHER WHEN SHE WAS A BABY AND WHEN SHE WAS 1 AND 2 YEARS OLD. WE USED TO GO TO REDFORD TOWNSHIP AND GO DOWN TO THE CREEK AND PLAY IN THE CREEK AND CATCH CRAYFISH AND PUT THEM IN A BUCKET. WE USED TO GO TO THE PARK AND GO ON THE MERRY-GO-ROUND AND THE SWINGS BUT JENINE HER FAVORITE THING WASNT A RIDE LIKE THAT

IT WAS A TURTLE STATUE MADE OF CEMENT 3 FEET TALL AND 6 FEET LONG. JENINE SHE JUST LIKED TO SIT ON IT AND PLAY NEXT TO IT. MISSY ALWAYS SAID THAT JENINE LOOKED LIKE A TINY MAGIC FAIRY GIRL WHEN SHE RODE THAT TURTLE AND I THINK MISSY WAS RIGHT SHE DID!!!!!!!! JENINE DOESNT REMEMBER ANY OF IT SHE ONLY REMEMBERS ME IN HERE.

JENINES MOTHER IS IN A PROGRAM IN FLORIDA AND JENINE LIVES WITH MISSY AND THAT IS THE WAY IT SHOULD BE THE 2 MOST IMPORTANT PEOPLE IN MY LIFE. I WISH THEY COULD VISIT MORE ONLY ONCE A MONTH. ITS A LONG DRIVE BESIDES THEY ARE ONLY ALLOWED TO VISIT ONCE A MONTH. WHEN I AM IN STATE ILL BE MUCH CLOSER AND YOU GET MORE VIS- ITS IN STATE. THEY WRITE ME LETTERS SOMETIMES EVEN JENINE WRITES ME LETTERS!!!!!!!!!! SHE IS SMART. I KEEP ALL OF HER LETTERS AND I LOOK AT THEM EVERY DAY 2 TIMES FIRST THING IN THE MORNING AND LAST THING AT NIGHT. I MADE A RULE ONLY LOOK AT THEM 2 TIMES A DAY THEN I HAVE SOMETHING TO LOOK FORWARD TO WHEN I WAKE UP IN THE MORN- ING AND LAST THING AT NIGHT. I LOVE JENINE.

MISSY IS MY SISTER. SHE IS 13 YEARS OLDER THAN ME. WHEN I WAS LITTLE I THOUGHT SHE WAS MY MOM. SOMETIMES SHE STILL THINKS SHE IS. WE USED TO FIGHT ALL THE TIME NOW WE ARE BEST FRIENDS. SHE WORKS FOR NORTHWEST AIRLINES SHE IS A BAG- GAGE HANDLER SHE IS TOUGH!!!!!!!! THINGS ARE

HARD FOR HER I WISH I COULD HELP HER BUT THINGS ARE HARD FOR ME TOO!!!!!!!!! I LOVE MISSY.

I WAS THINKING MORE ABOUT HOW DID I GET HERE. I THINK THERES A BAD PART OF ME. MOSTLY I AM GOOD BUT SOMETIMES I JUST GET A BAD NOTION. IM JUST SITTING THERE DOING NOTHING THEN WITHOUT THINKING ANYTHING OR FEELING ANYTHING I HURT SOMEONE BAD. THATS WHAT HAPPENED. IT WAS LUNCHTIME WE WERE EATING LUNCH. MIXER THATS THE FOREMAN HE WAS FIFTY FEET AWAY HE WAS TALKING A LOT. HES A ASSHOLE BUT NOT TOO BAD A ASSHOLE. WELL HE WAS JUST TALKING A LOT. NEXT THING I KNEW I PICKED UP A SHOVEL. NEXT THING I KNEW HE WAS LAID OUT COLD AND BLEEDING FROM THE HEAD ALSO HIS LEGS AND HIS CHEST WAS BLEEDING FROM THE EDGE OF THE SHOVEL. HE WAS HURT BAD THERE WAS A LOT OF BLOOD. EVERYONE WAS QUIET. I JUST WENT BACK TO WORK UP ON THE ROOF. THEN AFTER A HOUR THE COPS CAME. I DONT KNOW WHY THERES A BAD PART OF ME BUT THERES A BAD PART OF ME. THATS HOW I GOT HERE. I WISH I WAS A MAGIC STONE TURTLE.

WELL THATS ALL I HAVE TO SAY RIGHT NOW. IF THERES ANY MISTAKES SORRY. KIRBY FIXED ALL THE SPELLING AND I WROTE IT AGAIN BUT IF HE MISSED SOME SORRY.

A BLACK DOG

INSIDE OF TWO WEEKS Nicole and I had become inseparable. Each day went down the same as the one before, quietly magnificent. We'd wake up together, spill outside, and wrestle in the snow; she'd fix eggs or French toast while I entertained her in the kitchen; then we'd share a sofa and read for a while in musty morning light through the drapes. Later, we'd feed each other carrots and celery sticks at the fancy Lincoln Park cafés she favored and dash off to the afternoon movies or to the gym to play ball or down to the lake to check out the primate house and great cats at the zoo. Eventually we'd wind up back at her place, and we'd drink red wine, listen to old broken-down blues on WBEZ, and trade stories deep into the night, when we'd finally end up in her bed and fall asleep in each other's arms. As delightful a stretch as it was, there were moments each day tinged with sadness, since we knew time was short—I was moving to L.A. to scalp tickets at Lakers games, and Nicole's fiancé was set to return from his trip to Peru.

I'd actually met Nicole while I was hustling. Michael Jordan's retirement had been crushing for me and the rest of

Chicago's scalpers; without the Bulls gravy train, we'd been battling to stay afloat, working a nonstop string of concerts, theater, ballet, and pro-wrestling events, even shit like *Barney on Ice*. I'd finally given in and decided to head for greener pastures, though it felt odd to move cross-country for what was essentially a day job; scalping tickets was just paying the bills while I dedicated myself to what I considered my true calling—composing and choreographing an epic four-hour rap opera. The past three years I'd been dedicated fanatically to the task, but all my grand visions for it had crashed painfully down—Cali, I'd figured, would give me a fresh start all around. Hours after I cleared out of my rented room, at my very last scalping gig in the city—an Aimee Mann show at the House of Blues—Nicole appeared, a beautiful, exuberant girl pinballing up Dearborn Street, calling over and over, "Does anyone have an extra? Anyone have *one* extra?" We went to the concert together and out for drinks afterward, then went back to her place and stayed up all night perched on stools in the kitchen, dazzling each other with wild stories. At dawn, we made a plan: since someone was already moving into my room at my old place but we wanted to have more time together, I'd stay with her and her two roommates for a couple of weeks, then jet when her fiancé got back to town, which would still get me out to L.A. in time for the NBA All-Star Game. Nicole helped me carry in a few of my bags, which were already packed in my truck for the drive to L.A.—my clothes went into her room, the rest of it we jammed into a coat closet by the front door. She even cleared a shelf inside the bathroom mirror for my toiletries. It was like *we* were the ones getting married.

Nicole and her roommates had been planning a big party at the apartment; it happened to be the same night as my last night in Chicago. Half the city was invited. Nicole would have a chance to meet all of my friends I'd told her so much about, and I'd get to meet her man, a dude named Todd, who from his pictures looked like a decent sort—big, blond, oafish, the kind of sweet farm boy who played football in high school but always left the jock parties before they devolved into beer-swilling and date rape. Nicole seemed to love him but at the same time was aware that they weren't well-suited. Twice she'd put off the wedding, but she didn't want to break off their engagement for good. I told her I'd size him up and tell her what to do—I wanted to be brave and noble and advise her as a friend, not as a schmuck who was falling in love with her.

The day of the party I rushed around town saying 'bye to a few friends who had to work that night and wouldn't make it to Nicole's and taking care of all kinds of other last-minute shit for my trip. At a back-alley muffler shop off Diversey I grew sad. Snow dripped everywhere; a battalion of Puerto Rican kids raised my car on a rickety lift and scrambled around underneath, tinkering, tearing rust loose, and welding on new parts with a screaming torch that sent blue sparks scattering across the floor. I felt like every time I found a girl I got along with, some obstacle prevented us from really coming together—parents who forbid them to see me, a new job that whisked them off to Alaska, now a fiancé. Someday I'd find a girl with no strings attached who was down to roam the country and do art. I thought about the night ahead and dreamed that Nicole, faced with Todd and me in the same room, would have a wild moment of clarity and ditch him and run off with me to California. Anything seemed possible.

AROUND TEN O'CLOCK, I buzzed down to the South Side and picked up my scalping buddy Jay Johnson. He was forty and lived with his dad and six cousins in the Ida B. Wells projects. We'd been hawking tickets together for years, and even though we didn't hang out much outside of work, I knew I was really going to miss him. Heading back up-town, Jay leaned out his window at red lights to brush gusting snow off the windshield; my wipers were all iced up. We swung by Jewel Drug on Fifty-fifth Street to grab a case of Old Style, hopped back in the truck, and clattered up Western toward Nicole's place. "What's with this mar-ried girl you been hanging out with?" Jay asked me.

"We're just friends," I said. I was keeping it low-key; I was worried someone would give Nicole and me away in front of Todd and he'd melt into a murderous rage and wipe the floor with me. I said to Jay, "Besides, she's not married. She's just engaged."

"Yeah, Huey, whatever. I want to know what y'all two was *engaged* in last night when I kept calling your cell phone and leaving messages and you never called back!"

I broke down and told Jay everything. As far as I was concerned, I said, there was nothing really wrong with hanging out with girls who had a boyfriend or fiancé or whatnot. If they wanted to hang out, that was cool; obviously the dude didn't mean that much to them. Jay agreed, but he thought you were only shorting yourself if you got into a situation like that—a girl couldn't give all of herself if she was involved with someone else. That made sense in some ways, I said, but the way I saw things, once a girl spent some time with me, she'd tell other-man to get lost.

"But dude, hold on," said Jay. "If she's cheating on her current boyfriend, why you think she'll be faithful if she leaves him and she's with you?"

"First off," I told him, "she's not really the cheating type." Jay fixed me with a look. "No, I'm serious," I said. "She's not like that. See, it's like this—if a girl's got a boyfriend and she's messing with me, there's *something* she's not getting at home, right?" It could be sex, I explained, or simple affection, or even just a willingness on the guy's part to really listen. But if you gave a girl what she needed—if she was happy and really in love and not afraid to be herself—she wasn't going to be out running around town.

"Some girls are tricky, though," said Jay. "Some girls, man, they cheat no matter what."

"That's just girls with problems. They're afraid of getting too close. They try and sabotage a good thing when a good thing comes to them." Unless you like a girl driving nails through your heart, I said, you can't get involved with that.

Nicole wasn't tricky, she was just young and confused about things. Todd managed her dad's trucking company and her dad had set them up. It had the feel of an arranged marriage. Now she was unsure if she wanted to go through with it, but she felt a commitment to her dad as well as to Todd. It was a painful predicament for her and all very complicated. At times she grew desperate and hysterical; she told me she was trapped with no way out. In the beginning I just tried to chill her out. She was twenty-two, she was still in college. The whole world was open to her. I wasn't saying she had to get rid of Todd, I just couldn't understand why she'd go ahead and get married when she felt so conflicted. It seemed to me that if they stepped things down a bit in intensity and she didn't have this lifelong obligation looming over her, their relationship might improve.

At some point, though, during my stay with Nicole, I fell into a mad sort of love with her and no longer wanted her to smooth things out with Todd. Nicole was adorable. Her eyes roared with life. One minute she'd be deeply involved with her school books and the next she'd be balancing atop her chair, splashing wine from her glass, reciting some goofball inaugural address at full sweet volume; then suddenly subdued, she'd tell a mournful tale about a fight she'd had with her brother when she was eleven and he was eight, and she'd end in tears and come to me for a hug and a kiss, but a moment later she'd spring away and scold me for interrupting her studies, and she'd be back in her books as though her concentration had never been broken. I hardly cared what we were talking about, I just enjoyed watching her face. At night, close in bed, she'd chatter like a giddy teenager, then turn soulful and wise as we shared tales of sad things we'd seen. She felt everything deeply. Like me, she never fell out of love with anyone. She kissed with great feeling.

We hadn't made love—she was uncomfortable going as far as that with Todd's ring still on her finger—but in substitution we held fierce wrestling matches on her bed and walloped each other like merry adolescents. Occasionally, to provoke her, I'd call her a spoiled brat and a princess. She'd get incensed, and then when I told her how cute she was when she was mad, she'd really be furious. Nicole was tiny but athletic and strong, an accomplished soccer player and gymnast. A couple of times she pinned me.

I adored her—I loved her terrifically—but it didn't make sense to bother her with the news. She had enough to deal with as it was. I'd thought at first that all I wanted from Nicole was the chance to cheer her up for a couple of weeks so she wouldn't feel quite so alone in her troubles, and maybe in return an ounce of warmth and affection. By the night of the big party before I split town, I didn't know what I was going to do without her.

JAY AND I PULLED UP to Nicole's at ten past eleven and went inside. The place was a fucking madhouse. Bass shuddered the floor; pink smoke wafted overhead. In the entrance-

way, we cut a wide swath around two guys in dresses duel-
ing with fluorescent bulbs. It seemed like every artist, mu-
sician, and writer type in the city was packed in there,
along with a handful of scalpers huddled by the front door
talking shop, looking out of place. All around glimmered
the distantly familiar faces of people I kind of knew but
not really, the friends of the friends of friends. A total
stranger tackled me in a zealous embrace, calling me Gustav; I threw him off of me, fixed him with a squinting
stare, and played along, "Phil, you've changed, man! What
happened to you? Phil, you've changed." He told me his
name wasn't Phil, I told him mine wasn't Gustav; the
crowd carried us apart. Girls squeezed their way past, taking slugs off strange green bottles. Girls, girls, girls—they
were everywhere, dancing, shrieking, spinning; they were
up on each other's shoulders, chicken-fighting and blowing
bubbles. One had her shirt off. Over the din she pounded
a tambourine and insisted at the top of her lungs that
everyone start living life more simply so that others might
simply live. Jay shouted in my ear, "These white girls is
freaks, Huey! You really gonna leave this behind?" Just
then all the lights cut out. Mysteriously, within half a
minute, a couple dozen flashlights surfaced and everyone
was poking them in each other's faces like cops on a deliri-
ous manhunt. I couldn't believe this was the same room
where Nicole and I had chilled and played board games
the evening before. We'd had checkers and chess going at
the same time and *that* had seemed crazy. I was suddenly

afraid that in the hullabaloo I might not find her. I'd have to get on the road without saying good-bye.

Jay and I battled our way through the melee toward the dining room and the kitchen. Who were all these people? Where were my homies—Richie and Lu and Sarah and Steve? Things were a bit calmer at the other end of the party. I saw a few of the Logan Beach Café crowd. Nobody had realized I was still in town; I'd been too wrapped up with Nicole. I looked around but didn't see her anywhere. It suddenly seemed possible she'd blown the party off and was hanging out with Todd at his place. Then I heard her unmistakable laugh—sweet bells above the ruckus—and I wheeled around and there she was.

I wasn't prepared for the shock of seeing her with Todd. He had his arms around her. They were clearly a couple. Todd was a bear of a man, even bigger than I'd imagined—next to Nicole he looked ridiculous, oversized, an exaggeration of a human. He was pink from the sun and too much drink. Something else about him struck me as peculiar, but it took a second for me to place it—his head was humongous, way too large even for his hulking frame. Yet his odd proportions and his baby face gave him an innocence and charm. At once I felt sorry for ever messing around with his girl. Then an instant later I felt a stab of jealous outrage—what was this lummox doing with his arms around my dear sweet one?

Nicole beckoned me over. Jay hung close, curious, it appeared, to see how this little encounter was going to go down. Nicole burned me a look full of secret knowledge, but I was careful not to hold her gaze. The last thing I needed was for Paul Bunyan to get suspicious; I didn't want to arrive in L.A. with broken ribs and a busted-up face. Nicole seized my shoulder and said, "Huey, this is Todd, my fiancé." We shook hands; he gave a pleasant smile. "Todd," she went on, "this is Huey, the guy who's been our houseguest."

Houseguest? The word bashed at me and made my head hot, but how else had I expected her to introduce me? I'd dreamed that Todd and I were in competition—that I had a shot to win Nicole's heart—but the game seemed over before it had begun. I introduced her to Jay, fuming at myself for taking it all so hard. It wasn't like Nicole had lied to me and kept Todd a secret. With her usual gusto, she began an interrogation of Jay. Oh, she was sweet, a little mitey-mite packed with delight and wonder; I was drunk with love despite myself. Deep in me, volcanic forces rumbled, forging a kind of molten blade of determination that pressed out against my chest—I wasn't giving up nothing.

While Nicole and Jay bantered, Todd peered down at me from a great height. He said, "You're Claire's friend, right?" Claire was one of Nicole's roommates; apparently that was how Nicole had explained my stay to Todd—I was a friend of Claire's. That worked. It was discreet.

"Yeah," I told Todd, "Claire and me, we go way back. Like, super-far back."

He nodded. He seemed to remember more that Nicole had told him about me. "You're from Michigan," he said.

"Ann Arbor."

"Cool, I'm from Lake Orion."

"No shit? Is that in the U.P.?" I knew it wasn't, but I figured I'd get a shot in about him being from the boonies.

His good nature was unflappable. "No," he said, "it's like, twenty minutes from Ann Arbor. Right up M-23."

"Oh, my bad."

He wagged a finger at me. "You're the rapper," he said; he smiled a healthy smile, like it was a joke between us.

"I don't know. I was working on something . . . conceptual. It didn't work out."

"Well, Nic says you can really 'bust a flow.' You should go on tour with Puff Daddy and Eminem. But don't get shot!"

I didn't know what to say to that. Todd reminded me of all the small-town good Samaritans who'd helped me out when I'd had flats or run out of gas on some lonely country road and had used our time together as a chance to casually rail against blacks, Jews, and gays. I was sick of the small talk, upset with my own heart, aching to steal away for a moment with Nicole for secret kisses in the yard. A better man might have kept the conversation going, asked Todd about his Peru trip, his work, whatever, but I didn't have the energy. I cast about for an excuse to get out of there. "Hey Jay," I said, "let's put the rest of them Old Styles in the fridge." Jay was captivated by Nicole and didn't hear me. I pried the case from his arms, exchanged a couple last pleasantries with Todd, and headed away—not into the kitchen but back toward the heart of the party. I felt suddenly lonely and desperate, which meant it was time to get my game on and meet some girls.

HALFWAY DOWN THE HALL someone hissed my name. Nicole's bedroom door cracked open an inch. Eyes peered through from the darkness. I leaned in close. "Who's there?"

The door swung briefly open and a bunch of arms reached out and pulled me inside. The lights were off; I couldn't see a damn thing. Ten hands pinched my arms, my shoulders, and my neck. "We've got one!" one of my captors growled. "A skinny bugger by the looks of it."

"Put him in the brig with the others!"

"Toss him overboard!"

"Make him walk the plank!"

"Wait, wait. What's this, mateys?" There was a silence. "He's got beer!"

They rejoiced and clamored for my release. The lights came on. Everyone was smiling—Richie, Lu, Zach, Sarah, Kelli, Steve—my whole crew. The girls wore eye patches. "We set sail for the Indies at dawn," Lu explained. "We're hunting for doubloons." Zach and Steve toyed with fencing foils. Richie sat on the bed rolling a tremendous spliff.

It was a little complicated: these were my best friends, but they were also the ones I'd cast as the principals in my rap opera, and one at a time they'd deserted the project—all for good reasons, mostly that the opera sucked—but still there'd been some hard feelings, at least for me. Now, though, my relief at seeing them was so strong that any lasting soreness was immediately dissolved. I missed them already. For an hour or two we shouted and giggled at one another and sucked down cans of Old Style and got weeded out of our minds. At some point Jay slipped in. "That married girl's all right," he said.

"I know!" I said. I was high as hell. "I love her to pieces! I'm taking her to Cali with me."

"Yeah? What does big fella think about that?"

"Fuck that dude! I don't give a *fuck*. It's a free country, dog. Nicole, man, she can do whatever she wants to do." With that I banged out of the room to track her down. Across the party I spotted her, standing with Todd, tucked against him. With a monster paw he was squeezing her right breast and laughing about it—Nicole was laughing, too. Her eyes caught mine for a moment and sobered. Jolted, lovesick, and breaking, I turned to the girl closest to me, an underdressed little trollop with purple hair and fishnet stockings, and gave her an enthusiastic embrace and a kiss on the forehead, making a show of it. We started talking; her name was Sylvia. She claimed that in each of her previous incarnations she'd been a turtle—this was her first go at being human. I said I thought she was pulling it off fairly well. "I miss the water," she lamented. I suggested we hop in the shower.

I felt Nicole's eyes on me still and spent the next hour leaned in close to all kinds of girls—a vegetarian cellist, a cashier from Reckless Records, a cute bike messenger who

showed me her tattoos of George Washington and Abra-
ham Lincoln, one on each shoulder (never got the story on
that). I even started kicking it to Lu. "Girl, I ever tell you
how beautiful you are?"

"Huey, be quiet."

"Naw, I'm *serious*."

At last, Nicole worked her way over and bobbed up at
my side. "Nicole," I said, "this is Lu, she's one of my dearest
friends." Lu, looking perhaps to aid my cause, threw an arm
around my shoulder and gave me a peck on the cheek.
"Lu," I went on, "this is Nicole. I'm her 'houseguest.'"

Nicole looked distressed. I asked her how things were
going. "Things are great, Huey," she snapped in an odd,
happy tone. I couldn't tell if she meant it sarcastically or
not. Her eyes whirled like there were a thousand things
going on in her head. I was sore at her for her divided alle-
giance. The three of us stood in silence. Then Nicole
dashed off without another word.

It was almost four in the morning. Everyone was
pulling on their coats. Jay blundered down the hall, a pair
of pirate patches over his eyes. He bumped into me and
apologized, then realized it was me. "Hey, want to get
some Mexican food?" Sarah and Zach and Richie were
with him, along with a scalper we called Monet Joe; it was
cool to see they'd all made friends.

"I think I'm going to hang out here," I said. Past Jay,
down the hallway, I saw Todd stumble into Nicole's bedroom. Nicole stood at the far end of the hall, in the kitchen,

holding an empty bottle of wine and talking full-tilt to Claire while Claire's boyfriend, Nate Dogg, looked on.

"Okay," said Jay. "If I don't see you, have a good trip, man. Call me if you need money." He gave me a hug and asked me to aim him toward the front door. All the rest of them said 'bye and filed out after him and I was suddenly alone in the dark living room. Nicole's voice bounded down the hall; she sounded ruinously drunk. Her drunkenness depressed me. I'd wanted one last chance to really talk; now it looked like that would be a long shot.

I sat on the sofa and brooded on things and listened to Nicole and Claire. They were in the midst of a howling skirmish—some minor offense or imagined slight blown out of proportion by too much alcohol. These girls loved drama. Getting entangled with Nicole, it seemed clear, had been a mistake. I was fooling myself if I believed the two of us were going to sail off into the sunset—she wasn't ready to marry Todd, but at the same time she sure as hell wasn't about to give it a serious go with me.

In the kitchen Nicole and Claire began shrieking with laughter. Apparently they'd made peace. They came down the hallway hanging off each other. Nicole looked both happy and forlorn. Oh, she was truly a wondrous creature; in an instant I forgave her for everything. Perhaps we could curl up on the couch under a blanket, I thought, and kiss dreamily for forty minutes before falling asleep to *Fantasia*, as we had the night before. But without a glance at me, Nicole ducked into her bedroom and shut the door. Claire beckoned to Nate Dogg, "Come on, lover boy." They went off together and everything was quiet.

FOR A FEW MINUTES I sat there waiting for the next thing to happen—some passed-out girl left behind by her friends to wake up and creep from the tub; a gunfight between the teenage Cuban and Mexican gangs cruising Fullerton; sounds of fucking from one or both of the bedrooms. But the world was as cavernous and lonely and still as a baseball stadium in December. A great sudden sadness broke open in my chest. I winced at the pain and slid off the sofa to the floor, my heart mashed with jealousy and bitterness and longing. Orange light from the street flooded over me. Wind rattled the glass. I felt utterly lost and directionless. For years I'd been running from one place to the next—Chicago to D.C. to Maine, back to Michigan, a stretch in Tennessee, a mad dash out west to the Bay, then back to Chicago for a while. When would it stop? Why was I even going to California? I grew full of self-pity. I'd always figured that if I found the right girl, that would be enough to anchor me. The whole two weeks with Nicole, I'd allowed myself to imagine that I'd found a resting place. Jay was right—the situation was completely fucked up; I should never have gotten involved with Nicole; it was a sucker's bet.

I stood and wobbled to the window and looked out at the street. Snow billowed down in sparkling swirls—it was absolutely beautiful, and its beauty quadrupled my misery and made me ache for Nicole. She was twenty-five feet away and yet she might as well have been in a separate galaxy. I felt terribly sad. I felt betrayed by myself. I felt like the butt of a joke.

Just then, on the sidewalk outside, a black dog appeared, trotting and sniffing the air. It stopped right in front of the building, turned to look back, sniffed the air once more, then peered up at me. Could it see me through the window? I waved my arms around but it didn't seem to react. It was a big dog, a rottweiler or an Akita, the kind of powerfully built, no-fucking-around beast that all the drug dealers in the neighborhood kept on hand for status and protection. Around its neck was a collar and tags, so I knew it wasn't a stray, but it looked clearly lost—curled up, nibbling at its own paws, trying in vain to extract ice from between its toes. Periodically, it raised its head and looked around. Again it stared at the window where I stood, though it still didn't seem like it could see me. I looked around for my boots; I figured I'd go outside and help the dog find its way home. Then I had another thought. Maybe I could take the dog with me! I felt a great urge to rescue the sad critter, not only from the cold but also from an owner that would kick it outside on a night like this.

I pulled on my boots and was still looking out at the black dog when all of a sudden it cocked its head, lifted its ears as though someone was calling its name, and then jumped up and dashed off down the street and out of sight. I couldn't see or hear anyone out there, but I realized the dog must not have been lost, just out for a long walk off the leash. I felt strangely disappointed. Five in the morning; no one I could call and talk to, nowhere to go. Something like pride told me I couldn't sleep there on the sofa. I didn't have the heart to face everyone in the morning, deal with their jaunty chatter, smile with them, sit through breakfast. I wanted to just get on the road, but my stuff was scattered at a few different apartments and everyone was asleep; I'd have to wait till the next day. For a little while I tried to decide which of my friends would be the least aggravated if I woke them up and asked to come in to sleep on their floor. My truck, with the heat on full blast, was perhaps the best place to crash. I pulled on my jacket.

A door creaked open behind me. I looked around in time to see Nicole disappear into the bathroom. She was up—all right, I was going to talk to her. I tried to think of what I wanted to tell her, but there really was nothing to say except good-bye. A minute later she emerged. I didn't want to call her name out, in case Todd was up; instead I pulled a penny from my pocket and from across the room pegged her in the chest. "What?" she said, surprised and out of it.

I beckoned to her. She came over and stood close. "Thanks for everything," I whispered. "I'll see you later."

"What do you mean?" She was half-asleep and still drunk.

"Well. I'm leaving."

"What do you mean? I'm mad at you, you know that? I can't believe you."

"You're mad at me? That's great."

"You were all over those girls! How's that supposed to make me feel?"

I laughed. I hadn't expected this. "What the hell? You were all over that guy!"

"Todd?"

"Yeah. Todd."

"Well, that's Todd. That doesn't count." She glared at me and said mournfully, "You didn't even introduce me to your friends."

"I introduced you to Lu. Remember her? I used to be her houseguest, too."

"Huey!" she cried, delighted and exasperated.

I reached out for her; we came together and kissed. Life could be strange and lovely—things always worked out the way they were supposed to work out, but never the way I imagined. "Let's go for a walk," I said. "Look how beautiful it is out. Look!"

Nicole took a step back and gazed at the floor, bathed in sad orange light. A radiator down the hallway hissed and began to clang. For a moment Nicole teetered; then she looked up and said, "Good night Huey, okay? Just good night." She walked away from me, back into her bedroom, and shut the door.

I'd had enough. I snatched up my keys and barged out of the apartment. A cold wind blasted me; it was at most one or two degrees above zero, the kind of intense cold that cripples all hope. My cheeks and forehead burned; my eyes watered; miniature ice sculptures formed in my nostrils. By the time my truck heated up I'd be stiff as Walt Disney.

I realized I still had the keys to my old apartment on Kedzie Boulevard, a few blocks away. My roommates all still lived there, and I was cool with the guy who'd taken my room. I could just let myself in and sleep on the big brown sofa in the living room—it was more comfortable than most beds. Bracing myself against the wind, both arms in front of my face, I made my way up Nicole's street and at the corner hung a right toward Kedzie. White grocery bags bobbed past like ghosts. There was no traffic—no sound at all except for the creaking of ice-covered wires overhead. I imagined I was the sole survivor of a great apocalypse. Sadness lapped at me in waves.

At the boulevard the iron fence and tall snow-covered hedges next to the sidewalk trailed off, and as I turned the corner I came face-to-face with the black dog.

WE WERE BOTH STUNNED by the other. I let out a little cry and vaulted backward. The dog crouched on its hind legs in vague retreat, ready to defend itself. It eyed me warily, full of cold and weary disorientation. Steam puffed from its mouth.

"Hey there, dog," I said. "Come on over here, I won't hurt you. Come on, dog, let's get you home. Let me see your tags. Let's see where you live."

I took a few slow steps toward it. The black dog measured my progress and held its ground. It had short powerful legs, muscular haunches, a jaw like a bear trap. Yet its
eyes bore no malice. The beast had ice stuck in its pads
and it was lost and scared and far from home. Nothing
mattered more—indeed had *ever* mattered more—than
helping this creature. I kept talking as I moved nearer, as-
suring the dog that I only wanted to help. It seemed to
want to believe me but at the same time had been abused
too often not to be cautious.

When I came within a couple of feet, the dog cantered
back a few steps, showing off its athleticism and grace. I be-
seeched it to trust me. "It's okay, I promise you. I won't hurt
you. I promise." We negotiated in this way for a couple of
minutes. Every time I came too near, the dog backed off.
The snow was grainy and crunched under our feet like sand.

Finally the dog relented and let me get close. I felt I was
at the brink of a great, painful discovery. My heart thrashed
in its cage. The black dog locked eyes with me and for a
moment seemed to return my gaze with the same intensity
of empathy and compassion—we were both hurting, but
we were also now a tiny bit less alone.

Wrapped up in a rush of hot feeling, I reached for the
dog's collar. All at once its eyes changed and its ears flattened; from its belly rumbled a low mean growl. The trans-
formation was instant—once I'd crossed a certain boundary,
any bit of trust it had had in me dissipated like vapor. I
backed away. The dog moved toward me. It growled with

greater intention, its cleavered nub of a tail bent under. The night's dreamy mystery swirled away and my head was suddenly clear—I realized exactly what was about to go down. There was nowhere to run, no trees to climb, no fence high enough to keep me safe. My heart boomed. I thought of the word *mauling* and its hideousness. Protect your face, I told myself; if you go down, no matter what, keep your hands over your eyes.

The dog edged nearer and I kept moving back. I was careful not to make any sudden movements; I didn't want to trigger the attack. A wash of panic doused me in prickly sweat. This was all Nicole's fault, I thought. I'd have never ventured outside if she hadn't played me. Now she'd have to bear responsibility for my horrible disfigurement for the rest of her life.

I tried to remember the rule about looking a vicious dog in the eye—was that the way to assert dominance and cool them out? Or was that more likely to provoke them? Goddamn, I couldn't be sure. Dogs smell fear, I told myself. Don't act afraid. I pointed at the dog and said in the gruffest voice I could muster, "Hey—stay where you are— stay right there! You're a bad dog; you're a good dog; you're a *dog.*" If nothing else, I thought maybe I could confuse it. Then I stumbled backward off the curb and almost lost my balance and the dog tensed and dropped lower, ready to pounce. "No!" I shouted. The frantic tone of my own voice was about the most frightening thing I'd ever heard. Slowly, shaking a bit and breathing hard, I walked backward into the street. It looked like I might be safe, though. The dog halted its advance at the curb, content, it appeared, to let me make my escape. Relief swept through me. "Good dog," I said, halfway across, still facing it. "Now isn't that a good puppy dog." I was buzzing from the close call. Already, I imagined the whole thing as an anecdote I could relate to Jay or Richie in a letter once I got to L.A.—me, illing off girl shit and existential despair, looking for salvation from a killer canine who nearly shreds me to pieces. I turned away finally, gave the black dog one more glance over my shoulder, and hurried toward the far curb.

I hoped the front gate at my old place was propped open; in weather this cold, I remembered, sometimes the lock would freeze and I'd have to climb over. I wondered if anyone would be up, then thought about how late it was and realized there was no way. Right at that moment, as I reached the other side of the street, something made me turn, a sound perhaps—claws clicking on the pavement, a rough intake of breath—or maybe something more elemental, a primitive instinct not to turn my back on a predator. The black dog was in midair, a foot and a half from me, head cocked sideways, eyes beaded like a shark's, jaw unhinged. Black gums and white teeth; a soft deadly snarl.

"*No!*" I howled mightily. The dog seemed to react and draw up before it reached me. It barreled into my chest and slammed me backward into a signpost; I managed to grab on and keep my footing. The dog flopped off me and tumbled down and away. Its head caught a glancing blow from the edge of the curb and it yelped and wriggled to its feet. Blood pounded through my veins. I was ready for an all-out battle. "Bring it!" I cried, terrified, exhilarated, hungry to fight. "Bring it on, bitch!"

The dog took stock of my hysteria, unsure what to make of things.

"The fuck you lookin' at?" I screamed. "What you got? Come with it!" My head clanged. The night was roaring hot.

The dog took a step back. It watched me for a long moment with the surprised, quizzical expression of a parent whose child has just performed a stunning card trick. Then it sniffed the air with displeasure, sauntered off across the street at a long diagonal, and disappeared into a dark alley.

I STOOD REELING AND SHAKING, blasted with adrenaline. All at once I thought of Nicole sleeping peacefully in her toasty bed with no sense of my battles or the searing cold. I imagined Todd draped next to her, snoring, equally content. A surge of anger lashed through me: Why the fuck was I going to leave Chicago without telling Nicole how I felt about her? I couldn't skulk away, I couldn't surrender so easily; this was the time to stand up and fight! I had to put it all on the line, barge back into her apartment and tell her everything. Even with Todd right there, I'd just lay it down for her, let her know that I loved her, that I understood her, that we could be together—that we *needed* to be together. Maybe she'd leap desperately into my arms and tell me she loved me too;

maybe she'd scream for me to get out of her house; maybe Todd and I would scrap—I really didn't know. But already I was racing back toward her apartment, skidding on black polished ice, grabbing on to cars and fences and alley Dumpsters to keep my balance. My dashed hopes putt-putted bravely to life once more, like a bug that gets stomped on but keeps pulling itself across the floor. It occurred to me that if it wasn't for my encounter with the black dog, I would've just ended up creeping out of town alone. That's how the universe worked at times: little things—the *tiniest* things—could catapult you toward a good life, but you had to be open and you had to be paying attention. Love wasn't purely destined, it relied on hiccups of fate—Aimee Mann, someone else's trip to Peru, a black dog.

I spun around the corner toward Nicole's building and gasped—Todd was out front, in a red-and-black checkered lumberjack parka, big puffy gloves and no hat, taking hacks at an icebound car with a plastic scraper. Before he saw me, I ducked quickly behind a big frozen tree and looked on from the streetlights' shadows, trying to imagine what could have possibly forced him from Nicole's bed out into the bitter night. It felt like abacus beads were popping back and forth in my brain. Maybe they'd had a fight? Perhaps she'd told him about me? No, more likely, Todd had to go deal with some middle-of-the-night work-related emergency. I watched as he cleared a tiny porthole on his windshield; next he went at the side windows, gripping his scraper with both hands, stabbing and slicing away, grunting with the effort. There was something about his frenzy that actually served to calm me.

It drained the fury from me and I saw any conversation with Nicole for what it would be—sad, shameful, pathetic. If she'd wanted to be with me, we'd already be headed west. The fact of it tore a hole through me. Jay Johnson had always had a term for Bulls' tickets that for one reason or another he hadn't been able to sell: cardboard. Each time I'd given him a ride home after a game, he'd either smiled wide and flashed a bundle of c-notes at me, or fanned out all his unused tickets, given me the same smile, and said, "Look at this cardboard—a whole *lotta* cardboard!" I pulled off my glove and picked up a lump of snow. For all I'd sunk into Nicole, what was left was a whole lotta cardboard.

I left Todd there chop-chopping away at the ice on his car, and headed off toward Kedzie Boulevard and my old apartment. I was glad I had a warm place to sleep. At the front of my old building, I pushed through the gate, unlocked the heavy door, and stepped into the entranceway. It was hot as a sauna. I tore off my hat and scratched at the back of my head and my hand came back wet with blood from where I'd banged it against the sign post—the black dog had left its mark on me. I crept into the apartment like a thief. Everything smelled the same. The warped floorboards welcomed me with a familiar creak. In the living room, the TV was on loud; strange bursts of color strobed toward me down the long hallway.

"Hello?" a guy called. Then, quieter, "Griff, you hear someone come in?"

"Yeah. Santa Claus. He's two months late."

I walked down the hall and poked my head into the living room. People were crashed out two or three to a sofa and all across the floor. Tim Bisig, who'd taken my room when I moved out, peered at me through a haze of cigarette smoke. "Huey? Is that you?"

He and Griffin Rodriguez were the only folks still awake. They were watching *Babe 2: Pig in the City*. I rolled my jacket into a pillow and stretched out on the floor and talked with them for a bit. I explained to Tim and Griffin about the black dog, and how I'd nearly been eaten alive, though even as I told the story I wondered if I had conjured the whole thing up, if I'd been screeching in the street, crashing my head into things, wrestling a black dog that only I could see.

But Tim piped up, "Yeah, it's fucking crazy, man. I've seen that dog running around loose all the fucking time. It's fucked up. I like dogs, but that fucking dog . . . shit."

"You're scared of a dog?" Griffin said.

Tim laughed. "You haven't seen this dog, obviously. This dog's a brute. Huey, man, I know that dog. Fucking hell-hound. Fucking Cujo, man."

"Scared of a dog," Griffin repeated.

Tim mashed out his cigarette. "Shut the hell up, Griff, and watch the movie. Wait. Right here's a good part. This is a good part right here."

I was going to California.

NEVERGLADE

My GRANDPA DIED on Valentine's Day; two years later, when February rolled back around, my grandmother was sounding pretty lonely and down, so I figured I'd go stay with her in Florida and give her some company and also escape from winter for a while. She lived in a sprawling, crumbling retirement community east of Tampa called Neverglade Village; the entrance was marked off Route 8 by a beaten wooden billboard of Peter Pan riding an alligator.

My grandmother and I had always got along real well, but there's a big difference between getting along with somebody and actually moving in and living together. All the same, things started off smoothly. I turned my grandma's study into a little bedroom and she was cool and laid-back and let me keep my own hours. We found ourselves a good routine. I'd stay up really late writing and reading and go to sleep around six A.M., then sleep till one in the afternoon. I'd eat breakfast while she ate lunch, then we'd hang out around the little pool shared by her building and the neighboring building—we'd play backgammon or talk or read. Then we'd have an early dinner, I'd drive to the park to play basketball for a couple hours, come home, and start my night of work—at the time, I was trying to write a one-man play based on the life of Denny McLain, who was a star pitcher for the Detroit Tigers in the 1960s but later ended up a con man and a thief. My grandma would watch TV till midnight or so and then come in to say good night. She was amazing, one of those old people you could really communicate with—she responded to everything with clarity and wit, and wasn't shocked by anything. I knew she was hurting, but she didn't like to talk too much about my grandpa. Sometimes she'd sock herself away in her room with the Home Shopping Network booming. Then other times she would talk merrily on the phone to her friends.

Neverglade Village was huge—an entire dilapidated town of sorts, encircled by a four-foot wall, which seemed designed not so much to keep intruders out as to keep its inhabitants in; foggy-minded seniors had, in the past, wandered off into the marshes, where real alligators lived. Some days I'd jog a mile to the main pool and fitness center. I'd never done weight training before, but I kinda got into it, pumping iron while the easy-listening station cranked out songs from *Dirty Dancing* over a pair of tinny loudspeakers. The three or four wiry, rugged-looking old-timers who hung out there intimidated me at first but then began to sweetly give me pointers on how to do sit-ups and lat pulls correctly. Walking back to my grandmother's apartment, red and yellow birds flapped everywhere, while cars crunched by at ten miles an hour down the white-gravel Neverglade alleyways. It was such a strange, controlled environment, but it was weird how quickly I got used to the mildness and hush of everything. When I left to play basketball or get groceries, everything beyond the Peter Pan billboard at the front gate felt overstimulating, harsh, cacophonous. It was only ten miles to the ocean, but I hardly ever went—better to hang out by the pool.

A couple weeks in, I met Virgil, the guy in the apartment next door. He was ninety-one years old. His nose was bright red from decades of hard drinking and he wore a pirate patch where his right eye once had been—I always wondered but never learned how he'd lost it. Virgil was the kind of drinker who liked company to drink, and he'd invite me over in the afternoons and tell long stories and get me to match him drink for drink. By the time I got out of there a couple hours later I would be rocked. I'd be fumbling plates and knocking candles over trying to set the table for me and my grandma to have dinner. "You shouldn't let Virgil bully you into anything," my grandma would say. In return, I'd bounce around the kitchen and shout, "This food smells *delicious!* Yeah *boy-eeee*, let's get our grub on, *Grandmama!*"

I was having trouble getting any writing done so I started going back to Virgil's place at night, too, after I got back from basketball. His liquor cabinet was gigantic. He'd bring down a strangely shaped brown bottle and say things like, "Try this one, it'll put hair on your chest." Most of his stories were about his childhood in New York and his experiences in World War II in the Azores Islands off Portugal. His unit never saw combat. Instead they fought one another and the locals. His best friend was killed trying to jump a horse across a deep crevasse. His friend hopped on the horse and raced toward the gully, and at the edge the horse balked and his friend tumbled in. There was money on whether or not they'd get across—Virgil actually won money on his friend's death. He said he'd won a lot of money in the Azores betting on stunts like this and he'd sent the money home to his sister, who'd used it to open a hat shop that still existed under the same name fifty years later, though now it was owned by Nigerians. At some point, sometimes midstory, or even midsentence, Virgil would stand and disappear into a back room as though he was going off to take a leak, but he wouldn't reappear. I'd sit there for a few minutes, waiting for him to come back: finish my drink, gaze around the room for a while, maybe reach out and touch the texture of some of the various bottles that had moved from the cabinet to the table we sat at, and then finally I'd let myself out and go back to my grandma's apartment, where the Home Shopping Network was rumbling and every painting and bowl of seashells in the place seemed like the saddest thing on Earth.

My grandpa, we went to visit him a couple years before, a few months before he died—my mom, me, and my little brother. My grandpa had been deteriorating from Parkinson's for years, but things had gotten worse and we understood that this was the last time we'd see him alive. We watched a basketball game together on the little TV in his bedroom. Then my grandpa said he wanted to talk to me alone. The medication had him in a bad state and you had to get very close to make out his words. He told me that he'd been trying to figure out why God was punishing him with this disease, and that the only thing he could think of was that it was punishment for the fact that he hadn't insisted that me and my brothers get bar mitzvah'ed. I told him I thought that was bullshit, that it wasn't punishment for anything, it was just a disease. But he was certain. He pointed with his eyes toward a series of tomes on his bookshelf—a fifteen-book set called *The History of Judaism*. He told me his last wish was that I'd read it and learn the history of our people. What could I say? I told him I would.

When I was living there, sometimes I'd take a peek at those books and even take one down to the pool in the afternoon and make an earnest attempt to start reading, but I'd never get past page six. This other guy from the building named Dom would play backgammon with my grandma while I sat on one of the twangy deck recliners with the big tomes in my lap. I'd lay there with my eyes closed and listen to their small talk. Dom was kind and liked to tell jokes. His wife had died after a long illness a few years before. Whenever Dom talked about my grandpa, he called him Jay, which was weird to me because I'd never heard anyone call him by his name, they all called him Pa. Dom and him had been friends. Dom and my grandma talked and talked, then they'd lapse into silence and there'd be only the sound of dice rolling and backgammon tiles clicking against each other, and maybe, distantly, a sound from the outside world, from the high school that was nestled against Neverglade's walls—a car door slamming shut, a kid's shout. I'd drift off, and when I woke up eighty minutes later, the big *History of Judaism* tome would've left a white square on my belly where it had blocked the sun.

One night in April—it was the night before my birthday, actually—Virgil and I had a long, late session. He was recklessly drunk. I'd been alternating between liquor and Slice, but I was still feeling the liquor. It got very late. Then suddenly I broke open or something. For all the stories Virgil had told me, I hadn't told him one thing about my life—not because I didn't think he'd be interested but more because I liked his stories and didn't feel like telling ones I already knew. But suddenly everything came pouring out of me. I told him how my grandpa had made me promise to read those books and how I was letting him down. I told him about having my heart broke in Scotland and how I was still in love with the girl years later. And the story of the last time I'd seen her, flying a hot-air balloon and crash-landing it. I told him about the pitcher Denny McLain and all of his bamboozlings and the ruined lives he'd left in his wake; I told him about stupid shit, like the day in sixth grade when David Pfeifer beat me up with a pair of nunchuks; I even told Virgil about the decades-old *Young Students' Encyclopedia* I'd found in the fitness center that day—*Volume 14, Negro to Pantomime*. The fact that I was

living so far from the world I'd known bore down on me
like a great weight. I felt as old as Virgil, and everything
that had happened in my life before Neverglade seemed
distantly in the past. I felt like a dude on his deathbed re-
viewing his life. I couldn't stop telling stories, and Virgil sat
there nodding and gnawing on ice cubes and fingering his
eye patch and pouring himself drinks.

Then, out of nowhere, a woman appeared in the doorway to the back hallway. I was startled into complete silence.
She looked to be in her seventies or eighties, and she had on
a long lavender-colored nightgown. "Come to bed, Virgil,"
she said. She smiled at me like a ghost might smile at someone who couldn't see them. She moved closer, right beside
the table, and I realized a strange thing: one of her arms, the
one dangling right in front of me, was a dark arm, and it was
not real. It looked like it was made of brown porcelain. It was
completely straight, and hung from her shoulder like a golf
club. I wanted to touch it. Who was this woman? This whole
time—three months almost—I'd had no idea Virgil was married. Was this his wife? And why had someone stripped an
African American mannequin of its arm and mounted it on
this old woman? What had happened to her real arm? And
where, for that matter, was Virgil's right eye? Really, wasn't
that the story I'd been waiting for all these hot late nights,
wasn't that the obvious riddle, the hook that had me coming
back for more rum and gin and scotch again and again? Of
course, I realized, Virgil knew this, and that's why he'd kept

me in suspense—he didn't want to lose his drinking partner. The woman turned and headed back through the doorway; as she turned the corner, her stiff arm brushed the door frame and made a soft clunk. Virgil stood and followed her. I sat at the table touching the bottles.

Then I whirled out of there back to my grandma's place. Heavy Home Shopping Network bass thundered out from under her door. I rushed right up to her door and raised my hand to rap on it but paused. The night felt tilted and wild. Finally I barged right in. Her bed was empty. In the light from the TV I could see a little. The sheets were thrown back and the remote was on top of the covers. She had her own bathroom and I thought maybe she was in her bathroom, but she wasn't. I went to her window, which looked out on the pool. All the deck furniture had been carefully arranged by the maintenance crew and glowed orange under tall lamps here and there. Then I saw them, standing still and very close together in one corner of the shallow end, underwater lights casting them in eerie, moving shadows—my grandma and Dom. They were a ways away, maybe a hundred feet, and it took a few moments for me to see what they were doing, and to understand that they were kissing. They were touching each other's faces with their hands. It was breathtaking. My heart blasted away.

I raced out of her room and went to mine and grabbed one of the big *History of Judaism* tomes and my keys, then grabbed a stack of six beach towels from the hallway closet and headed for the door. Halfway out, I wheeled around and went back to my grandma's room and picked up the remote and changed the channel to one channel down, which happened to be, I discovered, Nickelodeon. I left again, went to my car, drifted through the silent, forlorn Neverglade streets and out the west gate, and drove fifteen minutes to the beach. I stretched out in the cool sand twenty feet from the water and covered myself with towels. The ocean gathered itself and crashed mightily onto shore. All the stars were sparkling. I pulled out *The History of Judaism* and realized I'd grabbed the wrong book—what I'd actually grabbed was the encyclopedia I'd found that day, *Volume 14, Negro to Pantomime*. I held it in my arms and watched the ocean. Its power and majesty were utterly captivating. The tide took deep inward breaths and then unleashed itself, and every time the surf pounded down I felt the jolt in the sand beneath me. It was warm and windy. The Azores were somewhere out there. So was Scotland. I hunkered down in my towels. I guess I fell asleep, because a couple hours later I woke up to a purple dawn, and the ocean was absolutely calm. Over the course of an hour I watched the most beautiful, understated transition from night to day, as the sky changed from dark purple to dark blue to dark red to red, then to orange to yellow and to pink—and still the sun had not yet come up. A big white gull landed close by and we watched together as the sun broke over the edge of the horizon, red and searing, at which point the gull batted its feathers and cried out twice, each cry in two beats, like the words *Hap-py* and *Birth-day*. Morning set in.

MAGGIE FEVER

I LIVED WITH MY OLDER BROTHER and his wife in Gulfport, Mississippi, from when I was seven to fourteen years old, but then my brother got stationed off the coast of Bahrain and I got sent out to Albuquerque to live with my grandpa. My grandpa was a weird and scary dude; he hardly ever said a word, just spat and grunted. He looked like a tiny Viking—barely five feet tall, with beady eyes and an enormous, ragged silver beard with yellow stains. Three or four days a week he worked at the McDonald's at Central and Coal and I went to school; all the other days we went to the airport and returned carts. These carts, the way it worked was folks would put a buck in the machine and un-hitch one to push their luggage around in. When you returned them, you got twenty-five cents back, but most people just left them in the parking lot and drove away, so me and my grandpa would spend all day collecting them and pushing them back to the terminal, filling our pockets with the quarters that the cart machine spit out. Together we could make more than fifty bucks in a day.

There was no camaraderie between us out there in the blazing parking lots, no buddy-buddy, no whistling while we worked. I kept as far from my grandpa as I could. If he seemed to take notice of me, it was only to grumble about my laziness and long hair. My grandpa was sixty-eight years old but for some reason told everyone he was ninety, and he looked it, so they believed him. He wasn't even really my grandpa, but he'd raised my mom and my older brother, so that's what we called him. All he ever did besides work was read and listen to basketball on the radio and play with his cat. He loved his cat more than anything in the world. The cat was named Gilbert, and it was an old, scrawny, tiger-striped stray he'd found in the McDonald's lot. Gilbert strutted around the house constantly wheezing and mewling and my grandpa followed him from room to room carrying on the other side of the conversation. They talked about sports, the weather, the crystal-meth freaks that worked at McDonald's with my grandpa, and sometimes they talked about me.

Gilbert was sick all the time and required special foul-smelling potions to keep him going. My grandpa mixed these on the back porch and twice a day he had me hold Gilbert down while he squirted murky purple juice down the cat's throat with an eyedropper. Gilbert blamed me—not my grandpa—for medicine time; whenever he saw me he'd run from the room, or else stand there arching his back wickedly and hissing.

One morning, on our way to the airport in my grandpa's

ancient, clattering pickup truck, he cocked his head at me and growled, "We're not doing carts today."

"Then why are we going to the airport?" I said. "Or are we not going to the airport?"

My grandpa said, "We're going to the airport but we're not doing carts."

"Okay." I waited for him to explain. It was the middle of October—the night before I'd figured out that I'd been in Albuquerque for exactly two months, which meant I had thirty-four months left on my sentence before my brother came home and I could move back to Mississippi. "Wait," I said, bolting up in my seat, doing the arithmetic. "Am I going somewhere? Am I going back to Gulfport?" Maybe my brother had quit the navy, I thought, and come home to Mississippi. Or maybe my mom had gotten an early release, or maybe my dad had even drifted back from wherever he was. My grandpa didn't say anything and I took his silence as a no and sat back, disappointed. Then it occurred to me that I wasn't going home, but was being shipped off somewhere else, most likely Yuma, Arizona, where my grandpa's friend owned an emu farm. For two months I'd been telling anyone who'd listen how much Albuquerque sucked, but now the thought of leaving—being jettisoned again—lodged a lump in my throat and made my nostrils sting. I couldn't believe I hadn't been allowed to at least get my stuff together. Was my grandpa just gonna box it all up and send it on? I was furious and near tears.

Finally my grandpa gave me his Viking snarl, "Okay, listen.

Gilbert needs surgery. That's right. They're telling me it's gonna be fifteen hundred dollars. At the least. That's what they say." We were getting near the airport. In front of us, a plane shot straight skyward, catching a blinding glare from the morning sun. "Here's what we're gonna do," my grandpa went on. "We're gonna pull up at baggage claim at American. You go in and pull the first two bags you see off the belt, bring them out here, throw them in the back of the truck. Then we'll do the same thing at Delta. And then we'll go home. And when I say the first two bags, I mean the first two nice bags, bags that belong to folks with money. And grab ones that look like all the others, so if someone stops you, you can just say you made a mistake. Right?"

"Why can't we just do carts?" I said, though I was thrilled to be part of a heist like this, and giddy with relief that I wasn't headed for Yuma to tend emus. Still, I told my grandpa, we could return enough carts to get the money together no problem, we could do carts every day, I could miss a few weeks of school.

"Gilbert doesn't have a few weeks," my grandpa snapped at me. "We need this now!" He merged into the lanes for arriving flights and fixed me with a look of grizzled menace. "Nice bags," he said. He spat out the window then looked back. "Heavy bags. And *nice*."

AN HOUR LATER we pulled up in the alley behind our house and dragged the airport haul inside to my grandpa's hot attic bedroom—four big suitcases plus a little green back-pack. My grandpa was especially pleased about the back-pack. "That's the lucky charm," he said. "That's our ace in the hole. We're saving that one for last."

We hoisted the first suitcase up onto his bed and my grandpa fought with the shiny clasps for a moment, then disappeared from the room and came back with his ten-inch hunting blade. He stabbed the suitcase once, drew the knife out, stabbed it again, and sawed from the second puncture back to the first. Together we tore the case open and dumped its contents out on the bed—sweatshirts, sweatpants, socks, women's underwear, a red umbrella, a tennis racket, a couple of skirts and dresses, a couple pairs of shorts, a few pairs of jeans, and a little plastic case that held makeup and toiletries. "Fuck," said my grandpa. With his forearm he rubbed the sweat around on his face. "Come on," he said, "bring another one over."

The next suitcase was filled with men's suits and busi-ness papers. We tried the pockets of every suit jacket and every pair of slacks but found only business cards, pens, and paper clips. The third suitcase was lighter than the first two, which gave me hope that it might have some-thing besides clothes, but all it held was about thirty card-board tubes; inside each tube were architectural blueprints for what appeared to be an enormous mall. Gilbert stalked into the room, crowing loudly. "I know," said my grandpa. "You're telling me."

He brought the last suitcase over to the bed and squatted

on top of it, the same way I'd hold Gilbert down when we gave him his medicine. As my grandpa plunged his knife through the bag's black nylon skin and ripped into its contents, I wondered if he had ever killed a man before, and I decided that yes, he almost certainly had, but that it had probably been during World War II, when he was in the army, fighting the Germans in Africa. This revelation filled me with both greater fear of him and greater respect.

"That's what I'm talking about!" my grandpa cried suddenly. He raised a black Nikon camera high in the air like the head of an enemy soldier. Then he added, a bit more composed, "There's a whole bunch of lenses, too." I jumped up on the bed and helped him dig. There were two smaller cameras and some camera equipment—flashbulbs, film, two tripods of different sizes. In the little zipper pocket of a pouch filled with batteries, I discovered a wad of cash— ones, fives, tens, and twenties. My grandpa snatched the money out of my hand and counted it up. "Three hundred and thirty-three bucks," he said. "And I'll probably get a thousand for the cameras, and I can get a couple hundred bucks for some of these suits." He stuffed the cash in the breast pocket of his shirt and gave me a black-toothed smile. "You did good." His eyes shifted. "Hey," he said, "what's in that backpack?"

I scooped it off the floor and tugged it open. Inside were a couple of lined notebooks filled with writing, a sketchpad, a beat-up copy of *Guitar World* magazine, and a Walkman with a few loose cassette tapes. "This might be worth a few dollars," I said.

"Tell you what," said my grandpa, "you keep that stuff. You did okay today." He grunted and pivoted and clomped out of the room and down the stairs, Gilbert at his heels, wailing. I closed up the backpack and slipped it over my shoulders like it was mine. For a long time I stood there, looking over the carnage of the four suitcases strewn across the bed and the floor. I heard the radio in the kitchen crackle to life—a noontime sports-talk call-in show—and the tiny, clanking noises of my grandpa preparing Gilbert a meal. Then the heat seemed to suck all sound out of the room. A powerful stillness descended. I became gently aware of my breath, and aware of the beat of my heart. The light through the drapes was red and soft and made the walls shimmer. Quarters piled on my grandpa's nightstand and card table and dresser and on the floor all hummed with a dull shine. I touched my face and found that I was crying. With my forefinger, I brought a tear to my tongue and tasted it—sweet, salty, hot as a raindrop. That was the first time I'd ever done that; now I always taste my tears.

MUCH LATER, after the sun had gone down and left the city smoldering, I walked out of the house and headed down Central Avenue a ways toward the McDonald's where my grandpa worked; my grandpa was home asleep, but sometimes his boss there gave me hamburgers at the end of the night. I was wearing my new Walkman and listening to the tape that had been inside—a series of low, melancholy trance beats. The world around me crashed and surged in time with the music. I glided past all the pawn shops and gun shops and residential motels, action in each tiny parking lot. A hundred and five degrees, hookers out hooking in twos and threes, a stream of red brake lights in the near lane as dudes slowed to check them out—passenger-side windows open, one hand on the wheel, faces hidden. Lowriders rumbled with bass, kids shouted giddy threats from car to car in Spanish; lights slipped red to green, engines buzzed like saws. Every half-block white men like dead stalks—every last drop of moisture squeezed from them—poked skinny arms from the sleeves of their jackets to grab at my new green backpack and ask me for change. I wondered if one of these men was my dad, if he'd choose this night to appear. Long hair, matted beards, camo fatigues, logoless mesh baseball caps, purpled eyes, scars, black scabs and wicked burns, brown teeth, missing teeth—each face rocked me like one of the barroom-brawl punches or collisions with motorcycle handlebars that had caused all their damage in the first place. This had to be the saddest stretch of road in all of America. It was as if the country was deeply tilted, and Albuquerque was at the bottom corner; in time, the most lonely and desperate of drifters would always drift here.

At the McDonald's, I sat on the weedy cement in the back of the parking lot and listened to the Walkman and watched cars whirl through the drive-thru. The contents of the backpack called to me; I dumped the stuff out, shuffled through the cassette tapes for a minute, then started flipping through the composition notebooks. They were covered with punk rock stickers and turned out to be a pair of journals that belonged, according to the return-address labels stuck inside the covers, to a girl named Maggie Smith. With blue and black ballpoint pens, she'd filled page after page in wild cursive scrawl. The very first sentence I read pulled me right in: "Well, that stupid fucker died today." It went on from there. "I was in the room with him and he died right there in front of me. He was alive and then he was dead. Not like he was moving much anyway, but when he died he was just gone, and I was there in the room with a fucking dead body. My dad's dead body. I sat there for about twenty minutes. Then I called for the nurse."

I did what I always did when I picked up a book— skipped to the last page. The entry was from early that morning. She was talking about getting packed up, heading back to Albuquerque from wherever she'd been. "If there's one thing that's bound to improve my mood and my outlook on life," she'd written, "it's being stuck on fucking airplanes for ten fucking hours. Well, at least I'll be home and can get fucked up. And I can finally sleep in my own bed again. Or Noah's, if he still remembers I exist."

Before I flipped back to begin at page one, I fished another tape from the little pile and popped it in—this one
was labeled with a marker, SHITTY OPERA. But it wasn't
shitty at all, it was beautiful. A man sang. I cranked up the
volume and drowned out the sounds of rattling exhausts
and the drive-thru speaker.

Maggie's journals only covered a span of a few weeks.
She'd written with incessant detail—ten, fifteen, sometimes
twenty pages a day, two full notebooks. Reading them was
like being dunked right inside her head. She'd gone to
Maine for a month because her dad had cancer and she
wanted to be with him during his final days, even though
she hardly knew him in the first place. But what had
seemed like a shot at becoming friends, getting to know
each other a little bit, had become a disaster. The whole
time she was there up until he died, her dad had been un-
relentingly nasty—not grumpy and sour, like my grandpa,
but outright vicious and cruel. "You know, you're even
uglier than your mother was"—that's the type of shit he'd
actually say to her, which Maggie a few minutes later
would record into her journal. It sounded like about the
most excruciating, punishing stretch of time I could ever
imagine; I could understand how keeping her journal always close at hand had brought some relief.

For the most part, though, Maggie didn't write about
her dad, she wrote about Noah, her on-again, off-again
boyfriend. She fantasized about sex with him—the details
were so raw, I started getting turned on right there in the

parking lot. She wrote about Noah's hands, his arms, his chest. She dreamed of vacations they could take together. Then, in nearly the same breath, she'd write about what an asshole he was and how much she hated him, and plotted ways to destroy him. She didn't seem confused, just equally intense in her love and her anger.

I'd never been so riveted. Every page I read, I felt Maggie press closer and closer to me. Maybe it was the music—her tapes—mixed with all the low-riders' blue fumes, or maybe it was the simmering haze of Albuquerque at night, just being there in the deserted desert city so far from everything I knew, but I felt dizzy and hollow. Maggie's every thought, every one of her tiny hopes and fears and sadnesses, ripped at me and consumed me. I felt gripped with a wild, desperate longing to be next to her, to hold her in my arms, to listen to shitty opera together in her warm and calm bed. I wanted to reveal myself to her as clearly and honestly and crushingly as she was revealing herself to me, page after page after page.

It occurred to me that she'd been delivered to me, that the universe had guided us together. At the airport, there were a hundred little bags I could have snatched off the conveyor—what force had compelled me to choose hers? I'd never been superstitious, but I felt a wave of gratitude toward whatever spirits were behind this. Was she sixteen years old? Was she twenty-four? It was hard to know. Nothing in her journals pinned it down. My only clues to her daily life were that she was in school and hated most of her teachers, that she worked at a veterinary clinic answering phones and mopping up urine, and that she had a car. I guessed she was seventeen. I didn't even know what she looked like but I didn't care, I was achingly in love.

I finished reading the journals and turned right back to the beginning and read them all the way through again, then switched tapes in the Walkman and read the journals a third time through. I paged carefully through her sketchbook—filled mostly with intricate drawings of spiders—and even read her *Guitar World* magazine cover to cover. Just as I was about to open the journals again, someone yanked the headphones off me; it was like being jarred out of a dream. My grandpa's boss—a young black guy named Calvin—squinted down at me; behind him, the McDonald's was dark. "Didn't know you was out here, kid. We done threw all the burgers away." He shook his head. "I got some McNuggets, you want some McNuggets." A black Cadillac bumped into the empty lot. "Come on," Calvin said, reaching out his hand. "Get up. My brother and me, we'll give you a ride home."

OVER THE NEXT FEW DAYS, I slipped into a kind of Maggie fever. Cool, vivid visions of the future came to me—driving with her through the desert at sundown, sleeping next to her in the back of a truck, a billion stars overhead; the truck itself seemed to click and sigh. A night at a county fair, looking at rabbits in cages; they pressed wet noses to

our fingers through the wire. We floated for a long afternoon down a lush Texas river on blow-up rafts. We sipped
flat orange juice at a sad midnight diner outside of Baton
Rouge. And early one morning, we watched from the run-
way as a small navy plane touched down and came to a
stop and a door popped open and stairs folded down and
my brother's squadron filed down the steps, one soldier at
a time. "Is that him?" she said after each of them appeared.
"Is that him? Is that him? How 'bout this guy—is this one
him?" These crisp scenes were what was real to me; the
rest of the world faded into an underwater dream. Dimly I
was aware of pushing carts around the baking-hot airport
lots, sitting in algebra class, holding Gilbert down while
my grandpa gave him his poison, but I wasn't there at all, I
was with Maggie.

One night I discovered that the tape she'd labeled
SHITTY SHIT contained her own tentative fumblings on the
guitar. She'd play a couple lines from a Beatles or a Paul
Simon tune and then get tripped up and say, barely audi-
bly, "Oh shit," and start over again. I felt closest to her
when I listened to this tape; soon I stopped listening to the
others. I got to know all the moments where she talked to
herself. At one point she said, "I suck at this"; at another
point she said, "This is hopeless"; and near the end of the
tape she said, in a moment of sudden triumph, "That only
half-sucked!" I lay in bed for hours with her Walkman on,
listening to SHITTY SHIT and touching the pages of her
journals, feeling the ridges her pens had dug. Every time I

looked at her name on the return-address labels, a bolt of nervousness flapped from my belly up through my lungs— I knew I was going to have to make contact with her and the thought of that was terrifying.

My grandpa hadn't been able to sell the cameras from the stolen suitcases for as much as he'd figured. When he wasn't at McDonald's or with me doing carts, he wandered around the house batting at flies with his hunting blade and talked about robbing a pimp. He could see that something had changed in me. He thought I was on meth. One morning he pinned me down and started chopping off all my hair. I kicked and screamed and flailed my arms, knocking stacks of quarters everywhere. My grandpa pulled his blade back. He couldn't understand why I cared so much.

"Maggie likes my hair long," I said.

"Who's Maggie?" he asked, softening.

"My girlfriend." I knew it was a little crazy, but saying it out loud almost made it feel true.

"Oh." My grandpa bit his lip and thought about that for a minute, still kneeling on top of me. "Okay, then," he said, "let me just even it out." He went back to hacking at my hair and I tuned out, so that I was with Maggie again. Now we were at a drive-in movie, tossing popcorn up, trying to land it in each other's mouths. Light from the screen played color across her hair and her face. Movie voices boomed from a little speaker mounted outside her window. Maggie laughed, then drew back in her seat for a moment, and her eyes, wide and whirling, gathered me in.

LATE THAT NIGHT—after doing carts with the Walkman on, giving Gilbert his purple juice, and lying in bed reading Maggie's journals for hours—I tiptoed up to my grandpa's bedroom while he was asleep and snagged the keys to his truck off the floor. I rolled the truck in stealth halfway down the block before cranking the engine on and rattling down Central. I stopped at McDonald's. Calvin was at the drive-thru window; he had on a silver football helmet and jersey. He squinted at me. "Is *that* your Halloween costume? You look like you done got chewed up and spit out. Who gave you that haircut, Stevie Wonder? Hey, your grandpa know you got his truck? Look, we been closed for an hour, I ain't got no burgers for you. Want some Chicken McNuggets?"

"Sure."

"Going to a party or something?"

"I'm going to my girlfriend's house." As I said it, I realized that this was it—I was really going to Maggie's house—and a jolt went through me, but then I felt extremely calm. Calvin passed me a little ten-piece box of Chicken McNuggets and I pulled away.

It was Halloween night, two in the morning. Everywhere half-costumed revelers crept home. Ghosts and a samurai warrior waited at a bus stop; three witches crowded around an ATM; Batman and Bill Clinton tussled in the middle of the road. The drive to Maggie's street took less than fifteen minutes. I'd expected a house, but her address matched a wide, crumbling, three-story apartment building. I parked and got nervous again. What would I say to her? Where could I start? I felt sick. I grabbed the green back-pack and climbed out of the truck and stood in the street for ten long seconds, then climbed back in and sprawled across the seat, near tears. Finally I gathered myself. I re-membered something I had to do—I unzipped the back-pack and took SHITTY SHIT out of the Walkman and put Maggie's trance mix back in, just like it had been when I got it. She wouldn't have to know I'd listened to her tapes or read her journals, though one day I was sure I would tell her.

The apartment building had the look of a halfway house where I'd once visited my mom—a thick main gate of wire mesh with a mess of barbed-wire rolled at the top, all for nothing, since someone had propped it open an inch with a pizza box. The entranceway led through to a little gravel-filled courtyard with eight apartment doors, each numbered with its own reflective sticker. But Maggie's address label hadn't listed an apartment number. Cinders shifted in my chest; every sound made me jump. Back inside the entrance-way I found the mailboxes for the whole building—a few of them listed names, a few of them didn't, and there was no Smith. There was no way to know—she probably lived with her mom or another relative who didn't even share her last name. I felt hopeless and clutched at my butchered hair.

Someone crashed through the gate behind me suddenly

and I cried out in surprise—it was an old, drunk Navajo woman. I asked her if she knew where Maggie Smith lived. I said the name a few times and soon she was repeating after me, "Maggie Smith, Maggie Smith, Maggie Smith," but she had no idea what she was saying. She kept banging into walls and falling down. I helped her up. She barged across the courtyard and started hammering on doors, crying out now, "Maggie Smith, Maggie Smith!" She understood I was looking for someone. Doors opened and slammed shut. The old woman careened back and forth across the dirt.

Then I heard, from somewhere above, a little voice: "Hi, I'm Maggie." The world fell into a hush. I looked up but couldn't see anything except dark windows and the purple night sky. "Here, I'm here," she said. The voice was unmistakably hers.

"I can't see you," I called. The old woman, deed done, lurched back across the courtyard and out the front gate. "Hey," I said into the deep silence, "I've got something that belongs to you. Your stuff."

"That's my backpack. Is that my backpack?"

"My grandpa made me take it. To save Gilbert."

"Who's Gilbert?"

"His cat." I hadn't intended to confess everything all at once, but I felt I knew Maggie, and I had nothing to hide from her.

"Oh," she said. "Well, why don't you come inside for a minute? Wait, I'll come down."

I turned slow circles in the night, raked with chills, unsure which door would open. I thought of bolting off. Then I began to savor the moment, this tiny half-beat interlude before me and Maggie came face-to-face. It was like being perched at a swing's highest point back, waiting to rush the air.

A door squeaked open twenty-five feet behind me. Halfway in, halfway out, stood a middle-aged woman. "Is that—is this—does Maggie live here?" I said.

She moved a little further out into the light and peered at me and nodded. Her face was open and moonlike.

"Oh, well, I have her backpack. Could I give it to her? She was just talking to me out the window."

"I'm Maggie," the woman said. She stepped out of her door and craned her neck back to follow my gaze toward the high window. I looked up again, too. The sky rippled and the stars clustered in. I felt light. I felt far away from everything. "Well, come on in," she said. "Come on inside."

I followed her in. The apartment air tasted of damp earth and cigarette smoke. We went down a long, dark hallway into a little room with two couches and two TVs stacked totem pole–style with the sound off—on one a weatherman waved his wand, on the other, a black-and-white Frankenstein staggered down a hillside while lightning flashed and wild rain whipped around him. The woman kicked one of the couches and the cushions seemed to sit up and arrange themselves into the shape of a man. He had a mask of orange face paint and his hair was dyed green. "Noah," the woman said, "you got to wake up for this." She disappeared and came back into the room with a glass of water. "Here," she said, "have a seat and drink this and tell me how you ended up with my backpack. I thought it was gone forever."

My heart jangled; I felt immersed in flame. I started into the story—telling her about Gilbert and how he was sick and all—and then the fever sacked me and the world seemed to turn inside-out. In my mind it was three months later and I was collecting carts with my grandpa in the curling heat, my pants heavy with quarters. I was listening to Maggie's SHITTY SHIT tape with her playing the guitar. But I was also still there, talking to that woman in the den—everything had become layered, like two different movies playing on the same TV. It was all real and it was all happening at the same time. More layers spooled out—I was climbing into my grandpa's truck an hour later and the old Navajo woman was asleep across the front seat. Then I was back in the den, asking the woman for another glass of water. She brought her guitar out and was playing it for me and Noah, tapping a beat on its body, and singing tunelessly, "Hey, you've got to hide your love away. Oops. I fucked that up." It really was Maggie, I could tell from her voice. I asked how old she was; she said she was thirty-six. I asked the woman—Maggie—if I could keep one of her tapes; I lied and said I wanted the opera tape, then reached into the backpack and drew the SHITTY SHIT tape out and wedged it in my back pocket.

"What else can I do to thank you?" said Maggie. I was done with my story; the fever had cooled; we were in the den with the two TVs, but at some point she'd shut them off. "What would you most want? Anything, just tell me, out of curiosity."

"But I stole your bag," I protested. "I'm just giving it back."

"He did steal your bag," Noah agreed sleepily, his lids hanging low.

"And you gave me a tape," I added. "That's a lot."

"Yup, baby," said Noah, "you did give him the tape."

The woman stared at me with owl eyes.

"Well," I said, "I'd like to talk to my brother. But that's impossible." I explained that he was on an aircraft carrier—the *Kitty Hawk*—halfway around the world. Suddenly, unexpectedly, I was on the edge of tears.

Noah came alive. "That's not impossible," he said. "Calling him. A guy I work with, Frank Tavarez, his son's on a battleship somewhere, like Japan or Iran. They talk every few weeks. It's always in the middle of the night." He jumped to his feet. "Hold on, Frank's maybe up right now." He headed down the hallway into a back room and I heard the beeps of a phone being dialed and Noah's muffled voice: "Hey Frank? You sleeping? Sorry, man. Right. Yeah. Hey Frank, I got a question for you."

Maggie and I sat across from each other for the next twenty minutes, listening to Noah's conversations as he made one call after another; I could barely make out his words but I was hanging on every pause and intonation. At one point Noah came back in and asked me for my brother's full name and the name of his unit, then disappeared again down the hall. Here and there Maggie strummed her guitar for a bit and hummed, as though to gently accentuate the action in the other room. I was twitchy with nervous excitement. Every time I heard Noah dialing another number, I imagined my brother at a command post in some dark, hot room deep within his ship—the kind of red-lit chamber in submarine movies where people shouted things. I pictured a phone clanging to life in the middle of a vast circuitry board, and my brother picking it up and saying, "This is Mabry," the same way he'd answered the phones when he'd worked at Robért's Refrigeration & Cooling Service in Gulfport.

Finally, Noah sidled back down the hall, cradling the cordless phone between his ear and his shoulder, a strange smile on his orange-painted face. "We found him!" he said. "But your brother's actually not on the *Kitty Hawk*. He got transferred to a base in Greece. We're on right now with the front desk at his barracks, they're going up to his room to get him. It's past noon there, guess they had a late night last night. Life of a sailor, right? Here you go." He handed me the phone.

My heart flailed this way and that; the room rocked side to side. I pressed the phone tight to my ear and absorbed the quiet buzzing silence. Maggie took Noah's hand and the two of them watched me, hopeful, open-faced. For a moment, I thought of the Maggie Smith I'd expected to meet that night, the Maggie my age, and I wondered if I would ever find her, and if so, how and where and when it would happen. The silence on the other end of the phone dragged on. My eyes began to water again, and I turned my head away so Maggie and Noah wouldn't see me cry. "Is he there?" asked Maggie. "Did he pick up?"

How can I describe what that silence was made of? It was thrilling, awful, crushing. It brought every blow, every scrape, every nick, every pummeling that my heart had ever taken straight to the surface. I found myself gasping. All I wanted was to hear my brother's voice.

The rest of it is easier to tell—an hour later, at dawn, five-fifteen in the morning, I pulled the truck up in front of my grandpa's place, Maggie and Noah beside me. Maggie wanted to look at Gilbert and see if she could figure out what was wrong with him. But there was my grandpa on the front steps, cradling the cat in his arms. The cat was dead. We got shovels and piled silently, all four of us, into the cab of the truck—Noah at the wheel, Maggie next to him, then me, then my grandpa at the passenger-side window, Gilbert on his lap. We took Central to I-40 to the Turquoise Highway and headed up the back side of the mountain. We parked and hiked a long, long ways up, taking turns carrying the cat. Finally, we agreed on a spot and dug a hole. My grandpa, breathing heavy, spread out on his belly and lowered Gilbert in.

But that was all still to come. In Maggie's den, the silence on the phone hissed and rumbled and crashed in my ear—it's the silence I still hear, always in the middle of the night, when I'm walking down an empty highway, or rowing across the center of a lake, or holed up in the last, darkened Amtrak car, looking out the window at distant twinkling lights. Some call it longing; I call it silence. That night, though, on the phone, there was a clattering sound, a pause, another little clatter, and then I heard my brother's voice, clear as a trumpet: "Hello? Hello? Anthony? Hello?"

ELENA

A FEW YEARS BACK I was staying in El Paso and I got low on funds. A guy I knew named Lance, who I used to do work for occasionally—patching up gutters, paving his driveway, that kind of shit—said he thought he could get me a good situation across the border in Juárez with a buddy of his. We went over on a Monday night and sucked down a few beers at a place outside of town called Las Placitas, one of those dank, drafty strip joints with rooms in back for fucking. Lance's buddy showed up. His name was Tony. He was about thirty, a wiry Mexican with gold ropes draped around his neck and a pink Diadora tracksuit that would have gotten him pounded or at least laughed out of any bar up in Buffalo. Here no one noticed, or if they did they kept their mouths shut, since he was the owner.

The three of us bullshitted for a few minutes and watched the show—a pear-shaped old hag shook her titties for a pack of shabby-looking locals at the front table. The place was mostly empty; weekends, Lance told me, they'd be rocking. Tony asked me a few questions, trying to get a fix on me, it seemed, make sure I wasn't border police.

Lance had already vouched for me, though, and the two of them were pretty tight; it wasn't long before Tony was outlining the details of his operation and what my job would entail.

Tony was a coyote; he'd smuggle folks across the border and on to any place they wanted to go—California, Denver, Chicago—for fifteen hundred bucks a head, kids under six half-price. Getting them over to El Paso was easy enough, he said, but on every road leading out of town there were checkpoints, and those were tough. Tony and the guys he worked with had begun to employ American truckers as mules. The truckers would pull their rigs into a motel parking lot in El Paso at three A.M., load the back or the undercarriage with fifteen or twenty illegals, and burn for Dallas or Amarillo. From there, Tony's cousins would unload everyone and get them to the Greyhound station and on the right bus to their destinations. The truckers made out all right, two to three hundred bucks per passenger, three to six grand a run. Even so, it was tough to find guys willing. The border patrol had caught on and become more vigilant, and the penalties were intense. The truckers knew they were playing Russian roulette; most of them would make a run or two, then quit.

My job, Tony explained, was to recruit the truckers. The idea was to get them out to his strip club, get a few drinks in them, let them at some free tail, then drop a few thousand cash in their laps—theirs to keep if they'd make a pickup the next night at, say, the Motel Durango on

Valdez Boulevard just east of Route 2. Each time they agreed—and made it to Texas without a hitch—I'd be five hundred dollars richer. I was twenty years old; I figured I had nothing to lose. I told Tony I was in. We shook hands; he gave me a grin full of teeth. Then he asked if I liked any of his girls—I was welcome to help myself.

I wanted to get out of it without raising suspicion and blowing my chance at the dough. "I don't mess with that," I told him.

"Okay, bro. Change your mind, just let me know."

Lance and I downed a couple more Coronas and split. It's funny—I remember I was good and drunk and so excited about the new gig and all the money I was about to make that I agreed to build Lance the shed he wanted next to his house for nothing, and when he dropped me off at the weekly motel downtown where I was staying, I called my sister in Buffalo and told her that in two weeks I'd wire her some money, enough for her to buy new school clothes for Stacy and Max and also to get her car up and running so she wouldn't have to keep taking the bus to work. My sister gushed all kinds of nice things. She hated taking the bus.

WITHIN A FEW DAYS it was clear that just about everything Tony had told me was bullshit. He didn't own the bar—it belonged to his uncle; he just ran the place. All that shit about the smuggling ring was lifted from somebody else's life. Even his jewelry wasn't his; it was on loan from a friend who owned a pawn shop on the U.S. side. The reason Tony needed me to bring truckers to Las Placitas was so he and his crew could get them drunk and then rough them up a bit, rob them of their cash and credit cards, and drop them off by the bridge, broke and bruised up. Running immigrants to Amarillo, the big ten-grand payoff— that was just the bait to get the truckers over to Juárez with their guard down.

Soon enough, it was obvious there weren't going to be any big jackpots for me, either. If Tony and his gang worked over one of the guys I'd brought in for a good score, they'd toss a few bucks my way. My drinks were always free. Women, too, if I ever got the urge. That was the extent of it. I had no other leads, no money, nowhere else to go. I figured I'd ride it out for a while and see what happened.

I started bringing in two or three truckers a night. I'd hang out at the truck-stop diners and bars on the U.S. side like I was some young rookie trucker myself and get talking to one of the guys about how I'd just pulled off a nice little side job and had come into a lot of extra cash. I'd play like I didn't want to talk about it but was so excited and proud I couldn't keep from bragging a bit. Finally, I'd break it down for them—twenty Mexicans in the back of their rig, three to six grand a trip; if they were interested, I knew some guys who could probably hook them up. No pressure—come across, talk to these guys, think about it. I got a good patter down, and besides, they'd all heard that other drivers were making money at it. One in three I talked to came with me. Every now and again I got a peek at them at the end of the night, bloody and beaten in a back room, or sometimes just passed out on a mattress with their underwear loose around their ankles. Most of them were decent guys whose only mistake was trusting me.

The more guys I brought in, and the more beat-up bodies I helped them haul out, the more heavily I started drinking. When I was too fucked up to cross back to the U.S. side, I'd crash on one of the nasty cots in the back rooms. Soon I was crashing at Las Placitas every other night, then five out of seven, then every single fucking night, and since I didn't have enough money to keep my room at the motel, I cleared my shit out and moved across the border, into this little storage shack behind Tony's house a half-mile from his uncle's bar.

Tony was a weird dude. When we'd met that first night he hadn't been outright lying so much as just caught up in all his fantasies of being a big-time smuggler. Night after night he'd get drunk off Miller Lite and bluster on about all the people he'd helped make it to the States. He was revered in Mexico and in the U.S., he'd tell me and anyone who'd listen. He claimed to have stacks of letters of gratitude from those he'd steered through safely. One time I heard him compare himself to the Statue of Liberty. He said people had cried when they'd met him, since they knew with his help they could finally realize their dream. He half believed the shit himself.

I got to know the hookers that worked for Tony. They

were a rowdy lot, cheery, hard-working, mischievous, sad. Most of them were between thirty-five and fifty, and they all had kids running around; some even had grandkids. A tiny makeshift village of shanties and run-down trailers out behind Las Placitas housed the lion's share of them; the rest stayed in the bar itself and its back rooms. In border towns, hooking is just a way people make a living. The women were working moms. Really, more than anything, they reminded me of my sister and the other waitresses at DJ's 24-Hour Diner back in Buffalo.

One of the ladies at Las Placitas had a fourteen-year-old daughter named Elena. Elena supervised all the younger kids down in the basement while their mothers were upstairs traipsing around onstage or in a back bedroom on all fours getting plowed from behind. I couldn't stand hanging out in the bar, so I started spending more and more time down below with Elena and her brood of munchkins. Elena was shy and sad and beautiful, with long dirty black hair and big brown eyes. She wore the same tiny Houston Astros T-shirt every day and baggy jeans with patches on the knees. As quiet as she was, she still commanded a powerful authority with the kids she watched over. When they got too wild, one word from her would silence them. She could break up a fight with a single stern glare. Of course it wasn't long before I was crushingly in love.

We'd have fun down there with the kids. Elena and I would split them into teams and for hours we'd play soccer, booting a flat mini-basketball around, dodging the iron posts. We'd sing songs. We'd tell ghost stories. It was like fucking camp. Every once in a while, Elena's gaze would meet mine and my heart would boom against my rib cage like a wrecking ball. Once a day I'd get her to smile, and maybe once a week to really laugh out loud, and for a moment I'd be soaring, happy in spite of my troubles, until Elena remembered herself and pursed her lips and looked sadly away.

One night when half the kids were asleep and the other half were busy torturing a rat they'd captured, Elena and I ended up close beside each other on a stack of old gym mats in a dark corner of the room. We talked in whispers; a tiny boy named Edgar was dozing at our feet. Elena told me about her dad. She'd met him only once, when she was seven—she and her mom had gone by bus down to Mexico City and stayed with him a few weeks. He was a welder. He had two sons that lived with him, brothers she hadn't known she had. "I wanted to stay there," she said softly. "But he didn't want." She traced a delicate finger down a long tear in the mat. "The bus ride back was the worst. We broke down. We were stuck in the sun. You can guess. I wasn't too happy." Her arm gently brushed mine and rested there so we were touching. A shiver raced up my spine.

Elena asked about my dad. I told her about the drugs and the drinking and all the rest. She laughed at the story of how I used to sneak him cigarettes when my sister and I would go down to visit him at the lockup in Elmira.

I turned to her. "What do you want to be when you grow up?"

Her eyes grew wide. "What do you mean?"

"I mean, what do you want to be? What do you want to do?"

"I don't know. What question is that? *What do you want to be?*"

"I want to be an astronaut," I said. "Or a fireman." She didn't know the English word *astronaut*. I didn't know it in Spanish. "You know," I said, "someone who goes to the moon. Explores space."

She nodded. Her eyes grew darker then brighter then darker again as sad thoughts streamed past like clouds covering and uncovering the sun. At last she said, "Soon I'll start work upstairs." Her words were like a kick in the stomach, though I knew at once I was a tool not to have already pieced together the obvious. "Like my mom," she added, in case I hadn't followed her drift. I was silent. I felt dizzy. Elena went on, "My mom is old. She can hardly keep working. I've got to do something. There's Ivan and Jorge and Matilda, you know." Elena had three young cousins that she and her mom looked after. "It's not so bad, they say. Working. Anyways, I think it's not so bad." She fell quiet.

For a minute we lay side by side, breathing, our forearms held together in a long kiss. My heart was sore. I loved Elena terribly. All I wanted was to melt into her. Music tinkled down from the bar above, men's rough laughter, the hollow roll of a bottle along the floor. The world beyond the basement seemed sinister and cruel and hot. I took Elena's hand. She wove her fingers through mine. A long, long time we lay like that; she fell asleep and I listened to her breaths and breathed in time.

I must have fallen asleep, too, because I was dreaming hard when the kids shook us, shouting in Spanish. Their rat was dead. "Elena, wake it up," they begged her. "Elena, Elena, wake it up."

TRUCKERS ARE NO DIFFERENT than doctors, lawyers, professors, or any other breed. Some are assholes, some are cool. Some run around on their wives, others stay true. The guys I brought to Las Placitas, though, one and all, were there for the pussy. The money, smuggling Mexicans, that was secondary. The pussy was the real bait. I made up all kinds of lies. They were in for the best pussy they'd ever had, I told them, the youngest pussy, the tightest pussy, the sweetest pussy. Soon they'd have enough drink in them, they wouldn't be able to tell the difference. The guys had stories for me, too—California pussy, South American pussy, Scandinavian pussy, pussy to die for. The odd thing was, a lot of these guys were loyal, devoted husbands and fathers. They loved their wives dearly, called them all the time from the road. They wouldn't dream of having girlfriends. A night with a hooker, though, was different. They weren't being unfaithful—the hookers were just an extension of their job, a way of relaxing after a long haul. In the same burst of thought they might tell me about their daughter's first hit of T-ball season and the Costa Rican whore with nice cans in Sacramento that they'd poked in the ass.

One afternoon I was hanging out at the truck-stop diner at Exit 19 where I met a lot of the guys I brought to Tony's when I saw a familiar face coming toward me. I froze. It was a trucker Tony's boys had worked over pretty rough just a week before, a dude from Tennessee, I remembered. I'd known this was bound to happen sooner or later but I hadn't figured out how I was going to deal with it. His eyes were beaded up, his chest puffed out. This was bad, bad news. I was ready to break for the door, but the guy barreled right past me without a flicker of recognition, then stopped two stools down and clapped another guy on the back and started palling with him. I got out of there quick. I knew I'd been lucky. One day one of these guys was going to want some payback, and they weren't going to go cruising around Juárez looking for the thugs who'd fucked them up. They'd come looking for me.

For a while after that I told myself that most of the truckers would be too embarrassed by their ordeals to mention what had happened to anyone. As long as I didn't run into any of the same dudes, I'd be straight. But I'd underestimated the speed at which information traveled at rest stops and travel plazas, in bars and restaurants, and over CB. Taking a leak one night at Whiskey River, a country bar in downtown El Paso, I heard two guys at the sinks talking. One of them knew a guy who'd gotten robbed in Juárez. "I guess some kid set him up," the guy said. "Told him he was going to hook him up with the coyotes, earn him a fast buck. Kid got him over across the river and the cholos took it from there. They got his wallet, his boots, everything. Even took his wedding band."

"Fucking Mexicans," said the other. He laughed mirthlessly. "They wonder why we've got fences up to keep 'em out."

Hearing those guys freaked me the fuck out but a few days later I was back at it. I tried out new places just to be safe—other bars in town, the casinos. I figured guys who liked to gamble might have debts and be more desperate for a sweet payoff, and that they might have more cash on them. Sometimes I just said fuck it and ended up back at Exit 19. Maybe I wanted to get caught, who knows? I was drinking more and more. I had a violent ache right between my eyes that never let up.

Now and then I'd have long talks with Elena's mom. She explained to me that until a couple years before, Las Placitas had been in Boys' Town and had been packed every night with gringos—college kids, truck drivers, doctors, lawyers, and professors. Most of them walked across from the American side, hailed a cab to Boys' Town, and got dropped off at Las Placitas' front door. But Tony always had a habit of robbing his guests. That didn't go over too well with the other club owners in Boys' Town or the cops and city officials in Juárez. They depended on American visitors and American cash. If Boys' Town got a reputation for being dangerous, things would shut down in a hurry. Tony and his uncle hadn't agreed to leave or to straighten up. Their place got burned to the ground. Two women died, and four kids. One was Elena's little sister. After a couple months Las Placitas had reopened outside of town.

Tony had a few cab drivers on his payroll who brought in white folks but for the most part his clientele was strictly Mexican. I made a lot of friends, drinking with them, but I was getting bitter on things and retreating. Some days I holed up with twelve brews and never came out of my little shack. I couldn't even be around Elena anymore. I loved her too much and the world was too hopeless.

Everything was in free fall. The beatings got worse. Tony and his gang seemed to live for that moment I'd walk through the door with some unsuspecting trucker—their faces would sparkle; they'd drink a toast to the ass-whupping that lay ahead. One night, after Tony and them had stomped a guy unconscious and dragged him out back, Tony invited everyone at the bar outside to take a turn pissing on him. I'd never seen men so gleeful. They shot guns off. They howled at the moon. Tony led the crowd inside, passed out a free round of Miller Lite, then brought them back out to piss on the guy again.

Another night, a guy I brought in saw Elena and got the idea fixed in his head that he was going to take her to one of the back rooms. Once he was good and liquored up and Tony's crew had him down on the floor, I whaled on him myself. My eyes burned, but for a moment the pounding in my head subsided. Tony and his boys cheered me on. All of them thought I was gay because I never wanted to fuck any of the women.

Then one time I ran in while they were roughing up a guy and tried to pull them off of him. I threw wild punches. I hit anybody I could. Tony and his friends just laughed and laughed. "Look, gringo trying to save his gringo friend!" They'd never seen anything so hilarious. Grinning, they shut me out of the room.

Day and night, a horrible screeching in my ears. I couldn't wait for everything to be over. I felt like a guy who'd jumped from a plane with no chute, watching the ground rush up.

Then I hit. I was drunk at noon, inside a dark motel room in El Paso with six big mad-as-fuck guys all around. I could barely piece together how I'd gotten there—tried to pick up some dude with the smuggling line, he was interested, yeah, had to go make a phone call, then wanted to stop by his motel.

I faced them. A couple I'd seen before. I'd brought them to Tony's. I could have offered some lame riff—I'd been set up, too, I'd had the shit kicked out of me by those fucking wetbacks, they'd taken all my shit, too; let's find those bitch-ass Taco Bell motherfuckers and kill them. But I didn't say a word. I closed my eyes and waited for them to strike. I felt weightless. I felt relieved. The first few blows stung but after that I didn't feel a thing.

NIGHT. I woke up in a heap of tires and broken glass by a pair of sweet-smelling Dumpsters. My face throbbed. My chest seared with pain, as though every rib was cracked. I was doused in gasoline. I couldn't make sense of why they'd let me live. Maybe none of them had had a match.

In a drainage ditch I washed off the blood that matted my hair and my face. My right eye was swollen shut. The world had fallen into a hush. I ghosted across parking lots and fields, dragged myself from one traffic light to the next, across intersections; I remember collapsing on a white convertible's hood, the bray of their horn. Then at last the bright lights of the bridge. I stopped halfway across, in neither country—nowhere at all—and slept on my stomach on the concrete; a boot in my ribs and a flashlight in my face woke me and prodded me to the far side. A cabbie who always hung out at Tony's gave me a ride out.

I found Elena; she wasn't surprised or alarmed to see me hurt so bad. She took me to one of the rooms in back to lie down. She lay down beside me. The moon crept over us. I held her close.

We kissed. We didn't say much. She touched my cuts. At one point I started crying and I cried for a long time. Elena kissed the tears from my eyes and my cheeks. She was crying, too.

I fell asleep again and woke up much later. The moon had set and pitched the room into heavy darkness. Elena murmured at my side, not English, not Spanish, a language of dreams. She was naked now. My hands traveled her body, across her tiny breasts, down her soft stomach to the downy softness between her legs. She pulled me to her and pressed her lips fiercely to mine. We kissed for an hour. The pain made me tremble. I loved her; I loved her; I told her I loved her. We made love quietly. The room filled with a sad blue dawn.

Voices sounded in the hallway. Elena and I clamped on to each other desperately, as though we could ward off the world and its sickness. Her heart chattered against mine. Out in the bar, the jukebox started up, and the music's clash seemed to wedge itself between Elena and me and drive us apart. She rolled away from me and we lay separate for a time. A red square of morning sun slid down the far wall. "I'll be right back," I told her at last. "I'm going to make 'em turn that shit down."

By the stage, at a table crowded with empty Millers, Tony and three friends sat drinking and playing cards. Tony saw me and called me over. He was gaunt and pale and whiskered, like he hadn't slept for days and hadn't shaved in a week. On the floor next to his chair, a girl, maybe twenty years old, lay passed out, naked from the waist down, legs splayed wide. Tony stood unsteadily. His chair teetered on its two back legs then crashed backward onto the girl. She didn't stir.

"Good morning, bro," said Tony. He took a step toward me, lost his balance, and caught himself on the table, knocking a half-deck of cards to the floor. His friends snickered and finished out their hands. Tony went on, "You know, I'm proud of you. All of us; we're all proud of you. Bro, you broke her in, right? You gave that girl a good dicking?" He laughed. "These guys thought you were a faggot. I told them no. I said, 'No, no, just watch. He likes the little one. He'll fuck her; give him time.'" He cast about for his chair so he could sit again, then saw it upended, on top of the girl, and decided to remain standing. "So? How was it? Was she sweet? Tell me that wasn't some sweet pussy." He kept on but I barely heard him. I couldn't stop looking at the girl under his chair. The thatch of hair between her legs stared me right in the face. Heat prickled up my neck, but as sick as I felt, I couldn't look away. "Listen," Tony was saying, "you did a good thing. I've always liked you, bro. You know that, right? Someone's going to fuck her brains out the first time, better it's you than any of these fucks"—he glanced at his friends—"and better than any of them gringos you bring in here." He looked at his feet and his eyes cleared. "They'll all get the chance, though. She'll bring good money, that's for damn sure." He was quiet for a moment, then he looked up at me. "Yo, bro, what the fuck happened to you? Looks like someone beat the hell out of you."

I was tired; I was empty. I had no fight left in me. Now, thinking back, I wish I'd broken a chair over Tony's head, smashed his face in, ground shards of glass into his eyes, forced a bottle down his throat. But that wouldn't have changed a thing. What I should have done is gone back to the room where Elena was sleeping and gathered her up in my arms and carried her far away. Where could we have gone? I don't know. It doesn't matter. We wouldn't have had to go anywhere. We could have barricaded ourselves in that little room, laid together on that sagging cot, and watched the days and nights flicker past until we melted into one, then faded into nothing.

But I failed her and I failed myself. I walked out of there, through the front door, into the rutted gravel lot. Once I got to the main road I broke into a run and I didn't lose stride until I'd made it into central Juárez, all the way down to the bridge. It was eight in the morning; there was a long line to get across—maids, cooks, dishwashers, and laborers with day-pass work privileges. I joined them. The sun rose up, white and hot. We inched toward the other side.

THE NEXT MONTH I stayed in El Paso. I built fences for people, dug holes, chopped wood, did some work on cars. Lance even paid me to build the shed beside his house. It was a strange few weeks—I quit drinking and had a lot more time to think on things, but was careful not to. I concentrated fully on whatever task was at hand—tearing a rusted exhaust from the belly of a Skylark, binding insulation to an attic ceiling, caulking tubs, slapping skinny nails into one-by-fours. When there was no work to do, I slept. I slept at the bus station. I slept in the park. Sometimes I went to the movies, sat in the last row, and slept in my seat. That month I slept twelve hours a day.

One afternoon, coming out of the movies, a woman stopped me. "Please," she said, "I need your help." I told her I was broke. "No, no," she said. "Please, listen, you're the only one can help."

Someone had told her that I was skilled at getting illegals into the country. She'd come down from Indianapolis to try and get seven relatives across the border and up to the Midwest.

"I don't do that kind of work," I told her. "I don't know who to put you in touch with, either." I said I was sorry, turned, and headed away through the parking lot.

The woman chased after me. She wouldn't give up. "You can trust me," she said. "*Please* help me. Please." There were tears in her eyes. I stopped and listened to her for a couple of minutes. Apparently she'd heard all kinds of horror stories about coyotes, guys who took the money and disappeared, guys who stuffed their stowaways in compartments so tiny that some died of heat and suffocation. She knew people who had saved for years to bring people over, then had the border police intercept them and, of course, the coyotes never returned any money if they failed to deliver. Somehow, though, she'd heard that I was different than the rest of the coyotes, that I was the best at the job, and also that I was kind and fair. It wasn't that odd, really. There were plenty of regulars at Las Placitas who could have overheard Tony's drunken fictions, known we were in league, and drawn their own conclusions. Then there were all the truckers who I'd spoken to and tried to bring over to Juárez who hadn't ended up coming with me. For all they knew, I was legit.

"I'm sorry," I told the woman. "I just—I don't know—I can't help you."

She tore open her purse and thrust a handful of pictures toward me. She started going through their names. I flipped through the pictures, half expecting to recognize one of them, but no, just a series of bleak anonymous faces, a couple children, a couple teenagers, a middle-aged woman, an old man with a gap-toothed smile—the same crowd I might have seen selling knickknacks on a side street in Juárez or on the corner waiting for a bus.

I passed the pictures back. "Look," I said, "I'm sorry, I really am. But I think you've got me confused with some-one else."

"I've got money," she said.

That stopped me. "How much?"

"Eight thousand," she said. "Almost."

"My usual fee is much higher."

"I know." She seemed both relieved and even more desperate now that she finally saw that she had my atten-tion. "I'll get you the rest of it," she said. "I have a good job. When they make it over, they can work, too. We'll get you the money. I swear to God, we'll get you every penny."

"Let me see those pictures again." I sorted through them,

and all at once I thought of Elena, and her mother, and her little sister who'd burned up in the fire. I felt things shift in my chest, and suddenly all the feelings I'd worked so hard to keep at bay those past few weeks surged in. I sucked in a ragged breath and dropped to one knee. Faster and faster I shuffled through the woman's pictures, not even looking at the faces, just flipping through them again and again, thinking of Elena, racking my brain, trying to work out a plan. I was shaking. Blood beat at my temples.

Then I knew what to do. I stopped and looked up at the woman. "Okay," I said. "I'll help you."

TWO HOURS LATER I was in Juárez, in the back of a cab, racing for the edge of town. The sun sank out of sight and the sky blazed purple and orange. As soon as Las Placitas came into sight, a knot lodged itself in my throat. All the front windows had been smashed in. The parking lot was empty, and here and there throughout the yard, charred tables and chairs lay strewn like bodies across a battlefield. I sent the cabbie on his way and dashed inside.

The place was in ruins. Glass splinters covered the floor and spray-painted messages spidered all over the walls and across the ceiling. Every room stank of beer and urine. At the stairs to the basement I paused. There were voices below. Hot smoke spiraled up.

In the farthest corner of the basement, I discovered huddled around a tiny blue fire of wood and bicycle tires as though they were the last human beings on Earth, I discovered four of the ragamuffins that Elena had always taken care of, hungry-looking, weary, and defeated. They were unmoved by my appearance, shy and a bit distrustful.

The boldest of them was Edgar; he explained to me in Spanish what had happened. Three weeks earlier the police had stormed in and hauled away Tony and his whole gang, and Tony's uncle, too, plus a few of the locals who were there drinking that night. Word came that they wouldn't be coming back for a long time. Hooligans from town broke in, finished off all the alcohol, and destroyed the place. One by one the women who worked and lived there picked up and left, taking with them whichever kids were theirs or had some affiliation. Edgar and three others had been left behind.

I asked about Elena. Edgar said she and her mother and her three little cousins had gone down to Nuevo Laredo, another border town five hundred miles to the southeast. One of the other kids disagreed. She said they'd boarded a bus south, toward Mexico City. I pressed them, frantic, hoping they'd remember more, but they grew quiet and pulled back into the shadows. Edgar asked if I was going to stay there with them. Now that I was there, he said, maybe we could play a game of soccer.

I'd lost Elena. Little muffled explosions rocked my chest. I felt panicky and wild, out of control of my thoughts and actions. In a daze I went upstairs and ransacked the kitchen. I fixed a huge pot of rice and called the kids up from the basement and watched them eat. My hands trembled. A great roaring had returned to my ears.

I told the kids I'd be back, that I was going for a walk, and I stumbled outside. The night was hot. Washed-out stars struggled against Juárez and El Paso's orange glow. I fought for breath, reeling, wounded. Every step took great effort, as though a terrible crushing weight had been placed on my shoulders.

A quarter mile into the hard desert I stopped, snaked a fist-sized rock off the ground, let out a cry from deep within, and hopped a couple steps and slung it as far as I could into space. A couple seconds later the rock came down not too far away with a single thud, and that sound was about the most final, sickening, hopeless sound I'd ever heard. I tore at my neck, at my eyes, at my insides. The roaring in my ears whooshed louder. I passed Tony's house—lights on, unfamiliar cars in the driveway. Black dogs in the yard hurled themselves toward me with muted barks and snarls; their chains snapped them back in midair.

I went for the shack where I'd stayed a couple months. I'd left all my shit behind. Inside, deep in the chill of darkness, I saw the red firefly tip of a cigarette, and my heart froze. I was not alone. For a long beat and a half neither of us moved or spoke. The roaring in my ears ceased all at once and I could hear the walls breathe and the windows sigh; then a voice broke the silence, a girl's voice, Elena's— two soft chirps in Spanish, "Who's there?"

"Oh, Elena!" I moved closer, ready to suck her into my

arms, but she retreated to the bed and stabbed out toward me with the hot end of her cigarette.

"It's you?" she said.

"Yes!"

She considered me in the pulsing dark. The wait was intolerable.

"Elena," I cried, "I came to find you. They said you were gone. I didn't know—I—but listen! I've got a plan now. I know what to do." I took another step toward her and again she moved back. She didn't want me near her, and I didn't know why. I was in agony. I wanted so badly to hold her, kiss her hair and her eyes and her lips, breathe her in. "What's wrong?" I pleaded.

Her cigarette flared. I saw her face, as though for the first time, and her beauty hurt me. "Sit over there," she said.

"What's wrong? What's happened?"

"Sit!" the hand with her cigarette dropped to her lap, and in its glow I saw that she had on a pair of my basketball shorts and the matching mesh jersey.

I sat on the dirt floor. I just wanted to hold her hand, touch her fingers, her wrists, the soft bend at the back of her elbows. It occurred to me that something awful had happened, that perhaps her mom and her cousins were dead. I asked her where they were.

"Nuevo Laredo," she said. "I'm going, too, in a couple days."

"Nuevo Laredo? How come Nuevo Laredo?"

"My aunt lives there."

"Ivan and them's mother?"

"No. A different aunt."

We were quiet for a moment. I tried to figure out how to say what I wanted to say. Finally, I began. "Look, Elena, listen, please listen to me. I don't know what's going on, but I need you to listen to me and hear me." I paused; the dogs in the yard wailed like wolves. "Elena," I said, "I want you to come across, I want you to come across so we can be together. I can get you across. I'm bringing a bunch of people over; I want you to come, too."

She was silent. A horrible chain of images flashed through my mind—Tony and his friends jeering me the morning I left, the last time I'd seen them, and all the empty Miller bottles, the playing cards scattered everywhere, the girl on the floor. I pictured Tony staggering out of the bar toward the back room where Elena lay sleeping, his friends right behind him, one of them holding her down while the others took turns with her. My whole body shook; I tried in vain to cast the thought away.

"Elena. Please. I'm sorry. Just talk to me. Tell me what you're feeling. Tell me you're all right."

"I'm all right."

"Good. Everything's all right, then. Won't you come with me?"

She pinched out her cigarette and there was total darkness. When she spoke she sounded tiny and far away. "I don't want to," she said. Her words landed one at a time, like four separate rocks scudding in.

"Elena. Tell me what you're feeling."

"I don't know what I'm feeling."

"Let me sit up there with you."

"No!"

"Hold my hand, then. Let's just hold hands."

She didn't say anything, so I scooted closer and reached for her. My hand found hers and grasped on. She didn't pull away, but just sat there with her hand limp, and breathed softly in the dark.

I had abandoned Elena; I deserved her uncertainty. I closed my eyes and focused on her touch. Perhaps she wouldn't have understood had I tried to explain it to her, but to me Elena was not only Elena—she was the sad-eyed love of mine who used to bag groceries at Woodley's in Buffalo; she was the sweet one who always sat across from me on the city bus in Niagara Falls; she was the girl I'd picked up hitchhiking in Mobile and dropped off in New Orleans, brash, full of sarcastic humor, but truly lonely and scared; she was the one I'd nabbed pinching Newports for her dad from the Marathon station I'd worked at in Bakersfield (I'd softened and paid for the pack myself); yes, she was the girl playing basketball with all the boys in the park, collecting cans by the side of the road, keeping secret pet kittens in an empty boxcar in the woods, walking alone at night through the rail yards, teaching her little sisters how to kiss, reading out loud to herself, so absorbed by the story, singing sadly in the tub, building a fort from the junked cars out in the meadow, by herself in the front row at the black-and-white movies or in the alley, gazing at an eddy of cigarette stubs and trash and fall leaves, smoking her first cigarette at dusk by a pile of dead brush in the desert, then wishing at the stars—she was all of them, and she was so much more that was just her that I still didn't know.

Slowly, timidly, Elena wrapped her fingers around mine. I could feel her beginning to come around, to let me in and open herself to my love. My heart filled with light. Warmth radiated from my spine and spread out my arms and legs to my hands and my feet, out to every finger and every toe. I'd never felt such a buzz of joy and promise. This was it, this was really it. My eyes watered. I'd loved her for so long—long before we'd met face-to-face—and now, finally, we would be together, together for good.

"Elena," I said. Her name itself thrilled me. "Elena. Elena. I love you."

There was a silence; the ground spun gently counter-clockwise. Then I saw everything as though from above, as if I was lifting off in a hot-air balloon—the dark storage shack; Tony's house, rectangles of light from the windows angled out into the yard; the dogs, their barks fading as they fell away. I saw Las Placitas, its empty lot, rubble strewn to the road. Higher, the broken-down homes at the edge of Juárez came into view, cars on blocks out behind them, and higher still, the pink argon streetlamps of town and pairs of headlights streaming through heavy intersections down near the bridge. Blinding white lights at the border crossing dazzled off the river, and beyond stretched the orange, amber grid of El Paso, pearled with traffic of its own. Mountains far to the west rose up like the rippled backs of black alligators. The Rio Grande laced its way out of them and across the desert, unspooling itself through twisting canyons and over the plains, marking the end of one land and the beginning of another, before at last, hundreds of miles to the east, it emptied into the Gulf of Mexico, a flat pool, black and reflectionless. From such a spectacular height, the river looked incidental, a near-imperceptible line of pencil drawn by a child's unsteady hand. Just as easily as it had been put down, it seemed it could be erased.

Elena peeped beside me and brought me back from space. I squeezed her hand and told her again that I loved her.

"I'm cold," she said. She pulled her hand away, and as she moved back on the bed and buried herself under the covers, I felt her part from me; it was like a continent cracking in two.

"Can I lie up there with you?" I asked her.

"No," she said.

I grew desperate. "Elena, I just want to lie next to you."

She said, "I don't want you to."

My heart flailed about. "Okay, I'll lie here, right here, next to the bed, right next to you, okay?"

"Okay."

"Let's talk. Want to?"

"No. I'm sleepy."

"Let's talk just a little. There's so much to figure out."

"We can talk in the morning."

I took a breath. "Will you come with me?"

"I don't know. I'll tell you in the morning." She said good night and she was instantly asleep.

That night was the longest night of my life. I rolled around on the floor, stomach torqued, pulse racing, and did more thinking than in all the years before and all the years since. I planned out ways to get Elena and the seven people from the woman's pictures across the river into El Paso. It was funny to imagine myself the next afternoon back at the truck stop at Exit 19, looking for just the right guy to carry them north. I thought of Edgar and the three kids still bunkered with him at Las Placitas. Couldn't I bring them over, too? But why? So they could hide out in basements of ruined buildings on the American side? My mind was a blur—I thought about rendezvous points and synchronized watches, Greyhound routes, the next week's weather, the work rotations of the border police, and when the best time might be to make a crossing. I thought of the money—eight grand—enough to cover the trucker, decoys at the river, tickets to Indianapolis, and more; Elena and I would have something to start on; I could wire my sister the money she needed for her car—she wouldn't have to take the bus again all winter.

Every once in a while, Elena turned over and made a soft sound in her sleep. I was dying to kiss her and hold her, miserable to be so far away. What if she told me in the morning she didn't want to come along? There was her family to think of; how could she leave them? No matter—if it came down to it, I would stay with her on the Mexican side. I fought with myself not to wake her so I could spill my heart to her and tell her every little thing I was thinking.

Each minute stretched for an hour. Now and then the dogs started up for a bit, then fell quiet again. I went outside to take a leak. There was no moon. A million stars blossomed across the sky. The world was still. I prayed for dawn to come.

Later, on my belly again on the floor, next to the bed and sweet-sleeping Elena, all kinds of memories suddenly avalanched into my head, things I'd never remembered before, strange vivid scenes, almost like dreams, except I knew they'd all really gone down, a long, long time before. Some were frightening, some were funny, and some were just there, memories of nothing at all—minnows under a taut lake surface, a yellow leaf stuck to a fence by the wind, the remote for the old TV in my dad's bedroom lying on the carpet, cracked open, batteries scattered across the floor.

I remembered a lot of shit with my dad—fights, yeah, but also a lot of good times, good times with my mom, too, and then all these adventures I'd had with Katie, my sister. One spring, when we couldn't have been older than seven and ten, Katie and I decided we couldn't take things in Buffalo anymore, we were going to run away. We packed bags with clothes and miniboxes of cereal, hopped a bus down to the highway overpass at Dove Road, and waited by the entrance ramp for a ride headed west. We wanted to go to California. Hours passed; we had our fill of Honey Smacks, Rice Krispies, Froot Loops, Corn Pops, and Corn Flakes. At last night fell, and Katie got cold and teary and wanted to go home. I wouldn't let her go. All night I told her stories about California and other faraway mysterious places— Mexico, Peru, Africa, Australia. I told her in the whole world there was only her and me, and that no matter what happened and where our travels took us, we would always have each other, I would always be there for her, she would always be there for me. In the morning, a state trooper in his squad car ground to a measured stop on the gravel shoulder, reached across the seat to roll his window down, and said, "Come on, you two, hop in. Your folks are worried about you." He let us ride with him up front.

The long night advanced. At some point during that blackest starless hour before dawn while I was curled on the floor, the wash of memories faded into dreams, and it was then, before sunrise, that Elena disappeared. I never saw her again.

SHOUTS

Thank you to my Miyagis—Charlie Baxter, Eileen Pollack, Warren Hecht, Judith Dewoskin, and Linda Baskey. Thanks to Blair Austin and Mike Kozura for getting me into this racket. Thanks to my folks, and to Brother Mike and Amy and Popcorn Pete. Thanks to Jason Bitner, Brande Wix, and Mike DiBella for always having my back. Thanks to Liam Murphy who put me up in the most beautiful house in America while I got these stories down. Thanks to Devin Friedman, Alex Blumberg, Tim-Pat Walbridge, Seth Meisels, Eldad Malamuth, Tim McIlrath, Tim Haldeman, and Rachel Frey for their generous encouragement. Thanks to Amanda Patten, Trina Rice, Paul Hornschemeier, and Jud Laghi for bringing this book to life. And most especially—thanks to you for reading it.

PEACE—DAVY